Celest

Every Day is Closer to the End

Riane Zháne

Thank you so much for taking interest in this project! I hope you enjoy it!

Riane Zháne Williams

Copyright © 2024 Riane Zháne Williams

All rights reserved.

ISBN: 979-8-9911501-1-8

Library of Congress Control Number: 2024917859

AuthorRianeZhane@gmail.com

Book Cover Artists: Cassidy R. Smallwood, Kaitey Collins

Crbuell013@gmail.com, collinskaitlynm@gmail.com

Thank you to Lilly, Nye, and Midnight.

Table of Contents

Chapter 1: Change 6

Chapter 2: One Step Closer 29

Chapter 3: Thirteen Years in the Making 45

Chapter 4: Break Away 63

Chapter 5: Someday 85

Chapter 6: Aren't They Beautiful? 94

Chapter 7: To the Moon 107

Chapter 8: New Beginnings 127

Chapter 9: All the Same, Nothing Different 155

Chapter 10: Reality 183

Chapter 11: Party for Three 209

Chapter 12: D'etre 227

Chapter 1: Change

Tears fall down her face like an endless sea. *Why do they always have to be like this?* Though she is trying her best to not listen, their voices continue to rock the house. *They'll stop, eventually.* Celest sits in the corner of her room. She tucks her head between her legs, trying to block out the noise.

She hums to calm herself. She slowly rises, her legs weak. *How long have I been sitting here?* She looks across the room at her bedside table. Her tablet stands on top of the many random items displayed there. Celest finds herself not having much energy to walk across the room. Reaching up, she knocks her tablet down, cracking its screen as it hits the floor. *What is wrong with me?* She rolls back over into a sitting position and turns the device on.

Celest tries hard but is unable to move. Her parents continue to argue over her silent cries. Her breathing slows and her heart rate falls soon after. There's nothing she can do. *They will never stop.*

The next thing Celest remembers is feeling warm and being held. She's still weak, but she feels gentle shakes, like bumps on the road. Her mother had been holding her for quite a while now. Celest and her mom are riding in a medium-sized van. The company Celest's mom works at sent the car to her after she called in. The driver never spoke, he was focused only on getting Celest in front of a medical professional.

Once Celest, her mom, and their driver arrive, and all the paperwork is filled out, the doctors start testing Celest for various things. After a couple of hours, they stop. Unable to find anything amiss, they send Celest to the hospital at once.

Celest's mom rushes back to the van, setting her inside. She tells the driver where to go and they take off.

At the hospital, they are instantly taken to a room. The doctors from the nursing office called the hospital right after Celest's mom left to let them know they were coming. Celest is laid on a bed and more tests are run on her.

After over four more hours of testing, the doctors finally come to an answer. They check her blood sugar. One doctor walks over to Celest and holds her hand. She pulls out a small clicker from the bag she is holding, placing it against Celest's index finger. Click! *What are you doing?*

Celest winces as the doctor squeezes her finger causing a small drop of blood to form. The doctor pulls out a small, rectangular device from the bag, puts something into it and then presses it against the blood on Celest's finger. Beep! *Why are you doing this?* She looks down at the device in her hands.

977

She shows it to the other doctors in the room who look shocked.

"Your daughter has Type 1 Diabetes," one of the doctors tells Celest's mom, "That means her pancreas doesn't produce enough insulin for her body to function properly. That's why," he takes the device from the female doctor and shows it to Celest's mom, "this number is so high."

Celest's mom grabs the sides of her chair, "Will she be able to live with it?"

The doctor nods, "Yes she will be able to live with it."

She relaxes her body a tiny bit, comforted by the fact that her only child will live past ten years old. All she can do now is wait.

The doctors hook Celest up to an IV. After spending the night in the hospital bed, Celest is moved to a hotel room connected to the hospital. Doctors zip in and out of the room twice a day to check her blood sugar.

942

896

830

Celest sits on her bed, playing with a set of Legos the hospital provided. The female doctor enters the room, sits beside Celest, and waves Celest's mom over. The doctor pulls out the same kit from before, "We're not going to be here for that much longer, so I have to teach you all how to use these devices."

She smiles at Celest, then to her mom who are both intently staring back at her. She pulls out the rectangular box and holds it up for everyone to see, "This is called a Personal Diabetes Manager or a PDM. You will always have to carry it and everything inside this bag with you. Its job is to tell you what Celest's blood sugar is," she pauses and makes sure Celest's mom is still listening to her. Celest is also listening, but at her age she won't understand everything.

"Then you have these," the doctor pulls out a small container, "These are called test strips. You put them inside the PDM so it can draw in blood. The last thing that goes along with this is a clicker," she holds up the device that pricks Celest's finger, "It is the thing that you use to prick her finger. You have everything so far?"

Celest's mom nods. The doctor smiles again and puts the things back in the bag. She hands the bag to Celest's mom, "We do things through an IV at the hospital, but it's a little different at home." She stands, walking to the small refrigerator that all the hospital rooms come with. She pulls two items out and sits back down, "This is a syringe, and this is a vile of insulin." She holds the items up to Celest's mom who carefully looks them over. "You're going to give her shots every time she eats and corrections every time her blood sugar goes high so we can avoid hospital trips in the future. What you're going to do is," she takes the top off of the syringe she is holding and pulls the plunger back, "fill this up with air and then stick it into the vile. Push the air out and then hold the vile upside down on top of the syringe." She pushes the air out and flips the vile over like she instructed. "Then you'll pull the plunger back out to the amount of insulin you need," she points to the little numbered marks on the tube, "You can use these to help guide you."

Celest doesn't speak but her mind is racing. *That seems hard. I don't know if I can remember all of that. The needle looks like it might hurt.* Her mom continues to talk to the doctor. Celest looks to her side. The Lego creation that she made earlier rests on one of the chairs in the room. She throws her legs off the bed and starts toward it. With nothing else to do, she takes it apart and puts the pieces back in their respective boxes. Her IV still follows behind her on wheels. She likes the faint squeaking noise the wheels make on the hardwood floor.

"I did notice that only you and your daughter are here," the doctor says, "This disease is a hard thing to work with and you're going to need support. Do you have anyone else at home that can help you out?"

Celest's mom hesitates before saying, "No. No one else can help me."

The doctor turns away, thinking, "Although this is not a free option, I am willing to pay for this on your behalf. I'm sure you've heard about diabetic alert dogs? There has been extensive research going on for the past few years to test how accurate diabetic alert dogs are and they were found to work over 80% of the time!" She pulls a pamphlet off the counter next to them and hands it to Celest's mom.

She looks over the booklet briefly but doesn't seem the slightest bit convinced. "You're telling me that you would spend all that money for me?" she pauses, "I heard they cost at *least* $8,000."

The doctor smiles again, "You won't have to pay a penny."

Celest's mom returns her gaze to the pamphlet and slowly flips through the pages. The doctor takes this time to entertain Celest. They spend some time rearranging the Legos into different animals and imitate each one. Celest takes a quick liking to this new woman.

Celest suddenly stops her imitation of the cat that she just built and lets her arms droop back to the ground. "What's wrong honey?" the doctor questions. Celest turns her head away. *Dad would never allow this would he? We'll never be able to get a service animal.*

"I'll take it."

Celest and the doctor snap their heads in the direction the voice came from. Celest looking more surprised than anything. The doctor simply smiles her sweet smile. Celest's mom continues, "Just let us meet him before we take him home. I want to make sure Celest finds a perfect match."

Dad is going to make us get rid of the dog. The doctor nods and leaves the room. Celest takes this as an opportunity to speak with her mother.

"You know dad won't let us have a dog," she says, "Why are you doing this?"

Celest's mom holds her daughter's head in her hands and responds, "Sweetie, I go through a lot of stress every day of my life. I'm going to take any help that I can get. This service animal is going to make sure you are safe and that's all that matters. Don't worry about your father."

That's impossible. Celest sits in the open seat next to her mother's chair. She stares into nothing for a while before speaking again, "How can you be so calm at home when dad acts the way he does?"

Celest's mom is surprised by her daughter's question. "Well, what do you mean honey?" Evelyn asks back to her.

"It's not that hard of a question mom. He obviously doesn't care about us, so I was just wondering what you do to calm down," Celest responds.

Celest's mom reaches into her purse and pulls something out. She explains, "This is a notebook that I've had since I was around eighteen. I had one before this, but I filled it up, so it sits at home in my bedside table. I write down everything in here, my thoughts, my feelings, how I view the world. It helps me sleep at night." She pauses and looks at the notebook in her hands, "You're right though; it's hard."

I should try that. Anything's better than what I do now. Celest looks away for a moment, lost in thought, "Can you get me a notebook?"

Celest's mom sighs, "I'm sorry that you have to ask me that. I'll get you one as soon as we get out of here."

I'm sorry. Celest leans back in her seat, preparing to take a nap. The doctor walks back into the room holding up a small stack of paperwork. "Sorry about the wait, I was trying to find the least excitable one out of the bunch."

Right when I was going to sleep. Celest sits back up and sees a photo of the dog. It's quite large for its age, has golden-brown fur, and the bluest eyes she'd ever seen.

"His name is Buddy," the doctor says, "He's around a year old."

She walks up to Celest's mom and gives her the photo to keep. "I can take you down to the adoption center as soon as Celest is discharged if that is ok with you," The doctor says before pausing, "My name is Marie by the way. I don't think I told you before."

"Evelyn," is the only response she got. Evelyn looks back to her daughter one more time before leaning back in her seat and closing her eyes. Dr. Marie takes the hint and gathers all of her things before leaving the room. Celest waves goodbye as she walks out the door.

***

"Do you understand all the requirements you need to take care of this service animal?" a male voice asks.

Celest looks over the man for the hundredth time. He's dressed in similar clothes to Dr. Marie; too fancy in Celest's opinion. It never made any sense to her. Why did people in good jobs have to wear such uncomfortable clothes?

Evelyn nods slowly as a hand rests on her shoulder. "It's ok if you need a moment. I can tell them not to rush you," Marie reassures her.

"I-I just..." Evelyn begins, but trails off, "I just don't understand why you are doing this."

"Just consider it me paying back someone I couldn't before." Dr. Marie looks to the man standing impatiently in front of them and quickly adds, "She understands. We will take excellent care of our new friend."

The man looks the doctor up and down for a little longer than usual, but eventually breaks his gaze. "Well then, follow me," he says.

The corridor they walk down is pretty narrow, white covering almost every surface they pass. *They should really change the scenery in here.* They continue walking until they end up in a round room with chairs lining the center in a ring of their own. People sit among these chairs with their new potential pets nearby, feeling them out.

"You can sit here," the man says as he points to an empty chair for Celest to sit in. "He's pretty calm, so there's nothing to be afraid of mom," he adds dully.

What an interesting place. I wonder how many people here are like me. Celest looks over her surroundings for a while. A little boy shakes nervously to the right of her while his mom attempts to calm him down. On her right there is an older woman who seems much too tired to be at a place like this. *I wonder what her story is.*

Before long, Celest is lost in her own observations. Only now does she realize how genuinely happy these people are. The older woman smiles, despite her restless face, as her companion is set in her lap. A boy grins after holding his cat's paw for the first time. Celest looks to her mom and sees her smile at Dr. Marie. *When was the last time I've seen that?*

And then of course there was her. She felt a warm feeling in her chest. A smile tugged on her lips as the man from earlier walked back in the doors with a retriever puppy in his hands, waiting to be received by her and only her. *When was the last time I was happy?* But no matter, she was happy now, so she decided to relish it. *All good things end, right?*

Evelyn is the first person to catch Buddy's attention. His head perks up and his nose sticks out to examine the new face. She chuckles at his behavior, before returning back to her solemn look. Dr. Marie pats the dog on the head and pets him a few times, smiling and small talking. Now, it is Celest's turn. The man bends down so she is on the same level as Buddy, allowing her to introduce herself at her own pace.

"Hello friend," she speaks softly. Buddy seems to have no reaction to the greeting, continuing to stare into

Celest's eyes. *What are you thinking?* As if able to hear her, Buddy scrambles out of the man's hands and into Celest's lap. He simply lays there for a while.

"You seem to pick them out right," the man says to Dr. Marie.

"Yes, Ben I suppose I do," Dr. Marie shoots back matter-of-factly.

"Come on," Dr. Ben says while motioning to the door, "Let's get out of here."

***

Back here again.

Celest stares at one of the superhero posters hung in her hospital room. It's not the same one; they moved her to a more comfortable room. She has a proper bed now, a kitchen area, and much more room. Evelyn is sitting on one of the lounging chairs, reading a magazine. Dr. Marie is busy watching over Buddy who sits in her lap.

Buddy turns his gaze over to Celest and jumps to the floor. He walks to her bed, propping his front paws on the edge. Dr. Marie smiles fondly at him, "He's saying that your blood sugar is high," she explains with a smile.

Evelyn looks at Buddy in amazement. Dr. Marie continues, "If Celest's blood sugar is low he will do the opposite. He will lay his paws on the ground and stretch out. He's also trained to wake you up during the night if anything is wrong."

Celest laughs at the dog's interesting behavior. Evelyn looks to the doctor and gently takes hold of her arm while asking, "Can I talk to you for a moment?"

The doctor looks back at her, concerned about what she has to say, but is hopeful. They walk to the other side of the room, out of earshot of Celest. *Good dog!* Celest slides out of the bed and onto the floor next to Buddy. His tail wags back and forth, thumping on the ground like a heartbeat. She pets the dog's head. *I hope you can stay with us.*

After talking for a little while, Evelyn waves Celest over. Celest stands and walks over to the pair while Buddy follows on her left side.

"Celest," her mom says, "this kind lady has offered to take care of you whenever I am unable to and help us out with your new condition."

Dr. Marie joins in, "Yes, your mother seems like a very nice person, and I want to help you both out in your situation. You'll be seeing me more often so you can just call me Aunt Marie."

Aunt? Celest nods at *Aunt* Marie. Evelyn must have noticed her uneasiness because she rests her hand on Celest's shoulder. "It's ok honey," she speaks quietly.

There's a loud noise, not quite an alarm but similar, from another room. Aunt Marie becomes alert, whipping her head in the direction of the noise. She quickly tells Celest's mom, "I need to go. Call me if you need anything Evelyn."

She bolts out of the room, leaving Celest and her mom alone again. "Celest, Aunt Marie says that we might be able to get out of here tomorrow," Evelyn says. *We can go home!* Celest smiles and hugs her mom. She asks, "Am I going to be ok when we get home?"

Evelyn looks at her daughter with weary eyes. "Yes, you'll be fine. I'm going to make sure of it," she says confidently.

The next morning went by quickly for Celest. Evelyn slept in the extra bed in the hotel room and Buddy slept on the floor next to Celest's bed. Celest is still hooked up to her IV, so Buddy's job was pretty easy that night. He still alerted Evelyn periodically that Celest's blood sugar was high, but she just gave him a treat and went back to bed each time.

There are various noises from the other hospital rooms; beeps, clicks, and whistles. *There's no point in trying to sleep.* She sits up, startled by how lit the room is, despite the hour. *The doctors still had to check on me. They needed to see.*

She looks over to her left and sees her mother sitting up, staring into nothing. She cautiously whispers, "Hey mom."

Evelyn almost jumps out of her bed before whipping her head in Celest's direction. "What are you doing up honey?" she asks.

Can you not hear how loud the other people's machines are? "I couldn't sleep. That's all."

Celest looks over her bed as she hears a familiar click, click, clicking sound on the floor. Buddy trots to the side of the bed and tries to jump up to Celest but hits his head on the guard rail and falls back down. *You're not big enough to make that jump.*

After recovering from his fall, Buddy settles for just sitting on the floor, again, on Celest's left side.

"Hey mom," Celest says, "What was his name again?"

Evelyn looks down at Buddy. "Aunt Marie says that his name is Buddy. It's also engraved on his medallion," she repeats as she points at Buddy's collar.

Celest jumps off the bed and bends down to Buddy's level. She holds her hand out and grabs Buddy's collar. She looks at the medallion hanging from it. *She's right.* "Buddy" is engraved in bold letters. Buddy, unsure what Celest is doing, licks her face. She laughs and releases his collar.

Celest walks over to her mom's bed, Buddy following by her side. She pulls herself up and sits next to her mother. Evelyn wraps one of her arms around Celest and tells her, "Any minute now we should be able to leave. We're just waiting on Aunt Marie."

Evelyn looks at Buddy again and notes, "He seems to have calmed down. He's not trying to alert you anymore. That means you're getting better."

Buddy sits on the floor and wags his tail. *You're always happy, aren't you?* Celest leans on her mom. *I hope we don't have to wait long.* Her wish ends up being granted.

Aunt Marie walks through the door thirty minutes later with a clipboard in hand. She announces in her peppy voice, "You guys sure are up early." She gives Celest and her mom her familiar smile and says, "Celest should be all good to go but I'm going to do one last check before you go home." Aunt Marie pulls Celest's kit out of her coat pocket. She asks Celest, "Would you give me your hand please?"

She holds out her hand so Aunt Marie can check her blood sugar again. Beep!

"You're all good! Now you just need to make sure that this number stays like this, ok?" Aunt Marie jests.

Celest and her mom nod.

"Buddy should be helping you out too, so don't worry," Aunt Marie says as she pats the top of Buddy's head, "Come on, I'll help you sign out." She walks back over to the door and holds it open.

"I'm here to sign Celest Whitfield out of the hospital," she tells the clerk at the front desk.

After looking at her computer for a little while, the clerk nods and gives Aunt Marie the ok to leave. Aunt Marie waves at Celest and her mom to follow her and leads them to the exit doors. "Is a ride here to pick you up?" she asks.

Celest's mom nods and responds, "Yes, he's in the black van right out front." She points to a car in the pickup zone of the parking lot.

I guess we have to go see dad now. Celest holds her mom's hand as they cross the street. Aunt Marie walks with them to make sure they get to the car safely. Once they get to the car, Celest's dad rolls down the passenger window.

"Hello," Aunt Marie says, "Are you taking these ladies home today?"

Celest's dad glares at Aunt Marie. He barks, "Yeah. Why do you care?"

Evelyn puts her hand on Aunt Marie's shoulder. "She was just asking. Don't make this a big deal," she tells Celest's dad.

Celest's dad shifts his glare over to Evelyn and says in the same rough tone, "Just get in the car."

Evelyn sighs and opens the back door for Celest. She points inside the car to tell Buddy that's where he needs to go. He jumps in, walking over the first seat, giving Celest room to sit next to him. Before Celest has a chance to get lifted into the car, Celest's dad notices that an unwanted being has entered his car.

"What do you think you're doing putting a dog in my car!?" he yells.

Evelyn is quick to react back, "This *dog* is going to help me keep our child alive! You would know that if you had actually came to the hospital when I called!"

There they go again. Celest's dad steps out of the car and walks around to the other side, where everyone else is standing. He insists, "I'm not leaving here with this stupid dog in my car!" He reaches through the backseat door and grabs Buddy by his collar.

Aunt Marie steps towards him, defending Buddy by saying, "Now, what do you think you're doing sir?"

Celest's dad ignores her comment. He yanks Buddy's collar, causing him to let out a small yelp, before tossing him out of the car onto the concrete. *I knew he wouldn't like Buddy.* Buddy hits the ground and rolls over himself before getting back up. He rushes back over to Celest, positioning himself into a crouch between her and her dad, and lets out a low growl.

"Oh look," Celest's dad mocks, "The little dog thinks it has a chance against me," he reaches down to grab Buddy again, but Aunt Marie intervenes.

She looks him dead in the eyes and screams, "Knock it off!"

Celest's dad stops reaching for the dog and stands straight up. Without another word, he gets back into his car and slams his door before speeding away. *He doesn't care about us at all. Now we're stuck here.*

Evelyn begins to cry, holding her head in her hands. Aunt Marie walks over to her, wiping the tears from her face. She reassures Evelyn saying, "It's going to be ok. I'll take you home."

Chapter 2: One Step Closer

"Won't you lose your job for this?"

Aunt Marie, keeping her eyes on the road, responds, "Don't worry about me. I have three other doctors who back me up. They won't be missing anything."

Maybe it's not such a bad thing that I'll be seeing her more. Celest sits in the backseat of Aunt Marie's car. Buddy lays to the left of her and her mother sits in the passenger seat. The hospital is about an hour away from her house, so they are going to be together for a while.

Celest looks out of the window to the passing trees and animals. *I've always loved the outdoors.* Celest's mom also looks out of her window at what passes by. Celest chuckles.

I must get it from you.

Aunt Marie grips her steering wheel, clearly upset. After being silent for a long time, Aunt Marie finally speaks up: "I'm taking you all back to my place. I don't want you around that fool."

Celest and her mom don't respond to her, continuing to look at the trees. *I don't care where you take us, as long as it's not home.*

Aunt Marie doesn't mind the family not acknowledging her. She tells them in a light tone, "I don't live far from your house. There's a pathway that runs through your neighborhood straight into mine."

Aunt Marie pulls into her driveway and gets out of the car. Evelyn follows, taking her daughter out of the car as well. Buddy jumps out and follows them as usual.

Aunt Marie walks towards her house. The outside is painted white. She has a small porch with a rocking chair resting on top of it. The pathway to the door is decorated with various pink and purple flowers. *I wonder why she chose this color.*

They reach the door which reads, "Love Benji." Aunt Marie opens the door and welcomes them inside. Celest walks in first and sits on the couch, followed by her mom shuffling in after her, looking down as she enters. "Take a seat," Aunt Marie tells her as she pulls a dining room chair out and motions over to it.

"Have you been diagnosed?" Aunt Marie asks unexpectedly.

Evelyn answers in a hushed voice, "What do you mean?"

"I'm a doctor," Aunt Marie responds, "You can't hide these things from me." She pauses to look at her friend's figure and explains that "You always look down, you have low energy, you don't look like you've eaten in days...." She trails off. Evelyn looks at her arms. Marie is right. She hasn't eaten in days; she was so worried about Celest that she hadn't been thinking of herself.

Aunt Marie looks at Celest. "That little girl needs you. You can't give up on yourself," she places her hand on

Evelyn's wrist and continues, "Evelyn, listen to me. I know you're going through a rough time, but I want to help you. I'm keeping you two here tonight. I have two extra bedrooms."

Evelyn snaps her focus to Aunt Marie's eyes. "I can't stay here! Richard will be so upset and there is no telling what he'll say about it!"

Aunt Marie gives her a small smile. "That's why I'm keeping you here. You need to stay away from him," she says calmly.

Evelyn gets up from her seat while slamming her small fists on the table, "I'm not staying here!"

What's going on? Celest freezes, craning her head to her mom. Buddy trots to her and puts his head in her lap. Evelyn slowly sits back down. Tears start to fall from her face. Aunt Marie gets up and walks to the other side of the table. She puts both of her hands on Evelyn's shoulders before taking Evelyn's hand and helping her out of her seat. Without a word they disappear down the hallway.

They will never stop. Celest looks down at Buddy. He looks up at her with his beautiful blue eyes. *I'm sorry that you got dragged into my life.* She pets his head. After a few moments Celest turns off the TV. *I'm tired of this.*

She stands, moving Buddy's head off of her lap. They walk down the hallway into the same room Evelyn and Aunt Marie are in. Evelyn lays in the bed and Aunt Marie tidies the room up.

Aunt Marie notices Celest and tells her, "Let's put you to bed."

She leads Celest back into the hallway, to the other bedroom. It's decorated with various flowers and toys. The flowers resemble the ones on the front porch. There's a bed and a nightstand on the left side of the room. Also, to the right, is a way to the connected bathroom.

Aunt Marie points to a pillow in the corner of the room, causing Buddy to rush over to it and lay down. She picks Celest up and lays her on the bed, tucking her in.

"Don't worry, it'll get better soon."

Aunt Marie turns off the light and walks out of the door.

The next morning Celest wakes up to something roughly nudging her. She sits up, letting the sheets roll off her chest. She throws the rest of the covers to the end of the bed and scoots her legs over the edge of the bed. *What is that bothering me?* She confusedly attempts to get out of bed to investigate.

Not again. Celest feels like a thousand gallons of water has dumped on her. Buddy jumps in front of her and starts whining. He bows to her, sticking his tail straight up. *What are you doing?*

He then runs out of the room. *Thanks for the help.* In a few moments he comes running back and does the same bowing motion. Aunt Marie rushes in the room behind him. After seeing his command, she runs out of the room again. She returns with a bottle of orange juice.

She hands the bottle to Celest and says, "Here drink only a little bit of this."

Why? Celest blankly stares at the drink offered to her. *What is this?* Her eyes slowly drift up to Aunt Marie. *Who are you? Why are you here?* Aunt Marie places the drink up to Celest's mouth and tilts it towards the girl. *Oh right. I forgot.* She finally drinks the orange juice slowly. Aunt Marie allows her to finish and sets the bottle on the nightstand, to her right. She grabs Celest's kit off the nightstand and pulls her PDM out. She sets it up, pricking Celest's finger and checking her blood sugar.

82

Aunt Marie sighs and relaxes a little. She looks down at Buddy and pats his head. "Good boy!"

She motions for Celest to follow her to the kitchen. She sits her down at the dining room table with silverware. Aunt Marie walks to the oven and fixes Celest a plate. She sets the plate in front of her saying, "Finish this."

Aunt Marie goes back down the hall towards Evelyn's room. Celest looks down at her plate. *Bacon and grits. This is nice.* She takes her fork and starts eating. Buddy sits to the side of her on the floor. *Do you want some?* Celest breaks off a piece of bacon and throws it in the air. Buddy jumps up and catches it in his mouth, smiling at her.

Aunt Marie returns with a syringe and an insulin vile. She walks over to Celest and sets the vile in front of her.

"I want you to watch this," she says.

She opens the syringe, performing the correct ritual for getting all the air out. She then sticks the syringe into the vile and sucks some of the insulin out. "You'll eventually learn how to calculate this all by yourself," she says with a smile.

Aunt Marie takes a step back and holds Celest's arm. *What are you doing?* She pinches a bit of fat from her arm and pushes the needle through her skin. *I don't like this.* She watches Celest's face, surprised that she hadn't pushed her away. After pushing down the plunger, she removes the needle from Celest's skin. She caps the syringe and sets it aside with the insulin vile. Although she did not protest, Celest looks to Aunt Marie with watery eyes. Aunt Marie notices, comforting her: "It's ok. You did great."

Celest makes her way to the couch, followed by Buddy who trots over with her, hopping on the couch beside her.

"I'm going to wake your mom," Aunt Marie says with a smile.

Celest nods at Aunt Marie. Within a few moments Aunt Marie is helping Evelyn down the hallway. *She's tired.* Celest watches her mom struggle to walk down the hall and into the dining room. Aunt Marie carefully sets Evelyn down at the dining room table. She quickly fixes her a plate and sets it down in front of her. Evelyn slowly picks up her fork and picks at her food. Aunt Marie brushes her hand against Evelyn's shoulder. She leans down and whispers something to her that Celest can't quite make out.

After Evelyn finishes eating, she gathers her things and walks to Aunt Marie. "Thank you for everything," she says in a hushed voice, "We really should leave now."

Aunt Marie gives Evelyn a blank stare. She eventually breaks eye contact and motions for Celest to get off the couch. She gets up, walking to the door. Aunt Marie opens the door for them, Celest and Buddy being the first to walk outside. *How strange.*

Evelyn stops for a second, looking back at Aunt Marie. "We just follow the path through the woods?" she asks uncertainly.

"Yes," she responds, "When you see the pond take the left path."

Evelyn turns away, walking down the driveway with her daughter and Buddy. They turn right and walk down the street, into the woods.

***

"Celest remember when I said I was going to get you a notebook?" a voice rings with false excitement.

Celest looks at her mother and gives a simple "Yes."

"Well, I think you should know how to use your notebook before I get you one," she responds in the same faux tone.

Empty promises, as usual. Celest ignores her mother and focuses on walking the path ahead of her. The trees that line the gravel are as tall as buildings. She listens to the songs of the birds that fly through the air. She also hears the scurrying of squirrels running away from them as her and her mother walk through the animals' home.

I don't want to go home. Evelyn looks out into the trees as well. She pulls out her own notebook and starts writing something down. *What are you doing?*

Celest gives her mom her full attention. *She's so calm while she writes.* Celest faces forward again. *But it won't last. Dad will always take it away.*

Not awfully long after starting their little journey, they run into the pond that Aunt Marie told them of. It is surrounded by various sized rocks. The pond itself is filled with lily pads and frogs. *This place is beautiful.*

Buddy runs over to a particularly large rock and sits next to it. Evelyn notices and stops writing. She grabs Celest's hand, curiously approaching the dog. As they get closer, they figure out why Buddy ran over there.

A sleeping foal is lying next to the rock as well. Buddy spends some time sniffing at the small creature but eventually returns back to Celest. Evelyn gets back onto the path, waves Celest over, and continues writing. *He likes animals too.*

Unfortunately, as Celest predicted, the nice thoughts don't last. The dirt path fades, and the trees shift into houses. The animals eventually silence. *Here we go again.* They live in an average neighborhood. Kids play in their yards and adults chat on their porches. It's something that has always bothered Celest. *There is no indication that something was wrong with their particular home. It just blends in with everyone else's.*

She looks up at her house while Evelyn approaches the front door. She holds her hand up like she's going to knock, but she pauses. Her hand suspends in the air. She looks back at her daughter and smiles. This is another thing that Celest never took a liking to. *Why fake it?* Evelyn leans over and kisses Celest on the forehead and then opens the door and steps inside.

Evelyn suddenly covers her face with her hands. Celest steps inside to see what's wrong. *Why can't I have a normal family?* Everything is gone. The furniture, pictures, *everything*. Evelyn breaks down on the floor.

She screams, "Why does he have to do this? Why is it always like this?"

Celest looks at her mom on the ground. *Please don't cry.* Buddy rushes in the door, lying next to Evelyn. He nudges her with his nose.

Do you think he left anything? Celest lets her curiosity get the best of her. She walks around the house, visiting each room, but she finds nothing. He even took the beds. Each room is a copy of the last; four walls and a ceiling, nothing else.

After making her way around the whole house, Celest returns to her mother. She's sitting up now, wiping her own tears away. Buddy is still resting his head against her body.

He's done this before, he'll be back. Celest looks to her right on the kitchen counter. There's a note on top that reads:

I'm tired of you doing things without my permission. I will not let some animal into my house. And since you decided not to come home, I've taken everything out. How do you like it when things are suddenly taken from you? You ruined my life, Evelyn. I never asked for this. I never asked for a child, especially not Celest. She is the worst thing that's ever happened to me. So now you know how it feels to have your life taken away from you. I hope you're proud of yourself.

I'm the worst thing that's ever happened to him. Celest steps back from the counter. *After all you put us through, I'm the worst thing that's happened to you?* Celest doesn't know what to do. She's too young to understand why her father hates her, but she never truly will. She doesn't know how to vent her anger because anger and sadness is all she knows.

She has had to grow up so much quicker than most people. Kids her age are more concerned with toys or playtime. All she wants is a family. A loving family. *If I could just take a step back and stop thinking about this, I would be happy. What kind of dad does this?*

I've sat in my room all day, for as long as I can remember, and cried. I cried like the little baby I was. No one cared what I thought. Because I had nothing else to do, because no one else cared, and because no one cared about me. And now, a few months later, with no help from you, I'm starting to understand. I know I am. And I will get through this the same way. Without you.

Celest walks over to her mother and flatly tells her, "Get up."

Evelyn looks surprised at her daughter.

Celest continues to stare down her mother with misplaced anger. "Can't you hear me? Get up," she reiterates.

Evelyn slowly stands on her feet. *You can't stand up for yourself, can you?* Celest aggressively hands Evelyn the note.

"I am your kid, and I am stronger than you," Celest says while walking around her mother.

"If you take orders from me, you will take orders from anybody!" Celest pauses to look up at Evelyn, "That's why dad uses you!"

She stomps her feet on the ground. Evelyn looks down at her daughter, still sobbing. She wipes as many tears away as she can, but it's no use.

Celest continues to shout at her mother. "I'm tired of this! I'm tired of you acting like you're worthless!"

Evelyn finally works up the courage to say something. "You're right Celest. It's always been like this," she pauses for a moment, "and it's not fair to you."

That's more like it. Celest's expression doesn't waver, and she doesn't shout while saying, "If you really care you will get away from dad."

Evelyn looks down in shame. "I would it's just-"

More excuses. Celest raises her voice again. "It's just what?"

"I-I just don't know how..."

Chapter 3: Thirteen Years in the Making

"So, tell me how it all happened."

It took mom three whole years to be able to ask for help. Instead of asking sooner, she decided to scrape together the little money she had and continue living in the barren house. I begged her every day to tell Aunt Marie, but she wouldn't listen. Sometimes I forget that my opinion doesn't matter. I used to think that when I got older, it might, but I was wrong. My opinion didn't matter then, and it never will. I just wish it didn't take me thirteen years to figure that out.

Aunt Marie faces Evelyn and Celest who are both sitting on the couch. *She's weak.* Celest refuses to look at her mother. Evelyn still makes an attempt to explain herself: "We got home, and everything was gone."

Celest turns her head to Aunt Marie. With the same stone-cold expression, she says, "He left a note saying how terrible we are," she hesitates, thinking about what she is going to say and comes up with, "and all she did was cry about it. I'm tired of this. Dad is going to come back one day and she's going to do nothing about it. Just like she always does."

Aunt Marie cuts her off. "Don't talk about your mother lik-"

"I wasn't done," Celest says while staring Aunt Marie down.

Unlike Evelyn, Aunt Marie is particularly good at discipline. She is not going to let a child boss her around. She sternly lectures, "Young lady I don't care if you're done or not. That is your mother, and you will respect her."

I'll respect her when she deserves to be respected. Celest sits back in her seat, biting her tongue this time.

"Celest let your mom and I talk for a little bit," Aunt Marie says, still clearly annoyed at Celest's outburst.

Celest gets up and walks into the room she stayed in before. Buddy follows her inside, carrying her bag in his harness. *She'll stop. She has to change eventually.* She walks over to the single window of the room. Outside she can see a view of the neighborhood and a few animals walking by. Buddy joins in, looking out of the window for himself.

Nature is beautiful. I just wish life was the same. Celest steps back, getting on her bed. She lays on top of the covers and stares at the ceiling. Buddy hops onto the bed, using the bench in front of it to help him. He lays down next to her, curling up.

Celest closes her eyes, listening to Aunt Marie and her mother. She can't exactly make out any of their words through the door, but she can hear enough to know they're not arguing. *That's a first.* At least thirty minutes pass before Evelyn and Aunt Marie stop chatting. *Silence.* A few moments pass and Aunt Marie knocks on the door. *What is it now?*

Aunt Marie announces, "We're going to go on a little trip. Get your things." Aunt Marie whistles for buddy, and he leaps off the bed. Celest stays put for a moment before deciding to follow Aunt Marie. *This better not take long.*

Evelyn, Aunt Marie, and Celest hop in the car with Buddy. Aunt Marie drives with Evelyn in the passenger seat. Celest looks into the mirror in the front of the car. "What are we doing?"

Aunt Marie stares back at her through the mirror and responds, "Don't worry. It'll be ok."

That's not what I asked. Celest relaxes, trying not to fight with her. She again looks out the window until they arrive at their destination.

***

Attorneys' office. Celest looks around the new building. Many people are in the waiting room who have already checked in. Aunt Marie holds Evelyn's hand as she walks up to the check in desk.

"Hello this is Evelyn Whitfield from over the phone," she says while gesturing to Evelyn.

The clerk looks at Evelyn and then at Aunt Marie. He types a few things on his keyboard and then hands Aunt Marie a receipt that prints. Aunt Marie accepts the receipt and walks over to the waiting area with the rest of the crew.

How do you think an attorney will help us? Celest sits at a chair near a bunch of magazines. Buddy sits to her right and Evelyn and Aunt Marie are at her other side. She picks up one of the magazines. *Tech and the Future.*

Aunt Marie notices her and chuckles. Celest darts her a look. *What's so funny?* Aunt Marie leans over, towards Celest. "What're you reading there?" she asks with a much lighter tone than before.

"A magazine," Celest replies bluntly.

Aunt Marie reads the first few lines of the page. "Can you read this to me?" she asks while pointing at the magazine.

I can read. Celest reads the magazine out loud: "In 2020 we should have flying cars. Along with this, predictions show that our AI intelligence will at least double by that time."

Aunt Marie smiles at her. *Surprised?* She tells Celest, "My son used to love reading things to me when he was your age."

Good for you. "I enjoy reading to myself," Celest mumbles.

Aunt Marie nods her head in approval. "Did your mom-"

"No, I taught myself." She flips the page and ignores Aunt Marie's gaze. "I was the one that read dad's letter to us if you remember."

Aunt Marie turns to Evelyn who looks terrified of her daughter's response. "She'll understand one day."

Evelyn lets a small smile cross her face as she returns her gaze to the ground. *You almost never smile.*

"Evelyn Whitfield?" a strange voice asks.

Celest turns to a man standing in the hall's doorway. He is around Evelyn's height and has a friendly smile. Everyone gets up and follows him into his office.

The man looks at Buddy. "Who's this?" he asks with a huge smile.

Aunt Marie answers, "This is Buddy. He's Celest's diabetic alert dog."

The man nods and turns back to the family. "I'm considering getting a diabetic alert dog for my son," he says in an even more excited manner.

I'm not alone. Celest looks down at Buddy. He looks a little uneasy, but he's not alerting so she must be ok.

"So, what brought you three ladies in here today?" the man questions, keeping his smile.

Buddy lifts his head and softly barks at the man. He chuckles and corrects his statement saying, "What brought you three ladies and this little guy in here today."

Buddy lays back down. *You seem like a fun guy.* The man smiles at Evelyn and Aunt Marie. Evelyn speaks up unusually. "I'm actually h-here for divorce proceedings," she explains.

The man's smile fades. He wasn't paying attention to it before, but he looks at Evelyn and notices how thin and shaky she is. He looks at Aunt Marie and asks, "Do we need to get the police involved Miss?"

"No, we don't need the police," Evelyn practically yells at the man.

We definitely do. Celest takes a moment to look around the room. There are various pictures of what must be the man's family, art pieces, and little artifacts on his desk. Among these are his nametag which reads, Robert Shaw.

Mr. Shaw looks down at Celest. *The kids always give it away.* "How are you going to go about handling her medical condition with your husband?"

Evelyn tenses in her chair. Aunt Marie holds her hand a little tighter than before. "I want to raise my own child. I want full custody," Evelyn says firmly.

Mr. Shaw stops in place and pries once again. "You have to have a very good reason to want full custody over her," he looks between the three of them, "Are you sure nothing is going on?"

There you go not standing up for yourself again. "He hits her," Celest interjects, "Well he used to anyway. We haven't seen him in the last three years."

Mr. Shaw looks back to Evelyn, who hangs her head. "I'm very sorry Ms. I'll get on your case right away." He asks for a few things like Evelyn's date of birth, where she currently lives, and so on. "Ms. Evelyn if you truly haven't seen him in that many years, he is very likely to not show up to court."

Aunt Marie questions, "What does that mean?"

"It means you will automatically win the case." Mr. Shaw goes back to typing on his computer. *We would win?* Celest drifts into thought again while Evelyn and Aunt Marie answer a few more questions.

"What is your husband's name ma'am?"

"H-his name is Richard." *You still have trouble saying his name.* Evelyn continues, "I'm sorry but I don't really know anything else about him. I don't even know where he lives now."

Mr. Shaw rests his arms on his desk and puts on a serious face. "Now this is what we're going to do. I'll run you guys down to the police station and we'll tell them what's going on. I'm going to help get you out of this situation."

Buddy suddenly pipes up and walks to the back of the room, where everyone can see him. He puts his paws down and stretches out. *That's not good.* Celest interrupts the conversation once again: "I'm sorry, but I think he's trying to say something."

Evelyn and Aunt Marie look down at Buddy. Evelyn looks to Aunt Marie for reassurance before reaching inside Buddy's vest to get her PDM. She pulls it out and tests her daughter. *I can do this myself now. I'm not ten anymore.*

80

Evelyn reaches in her purse to pull out an orange juice. She hands it to Celest and shows how much to drink. Evelyn pulls out a small bag of treats from her purse and tosses one to Buddy.

Mr. Shaw watches in amazement and his smile returns. "Well, you guys have got this down to a science!" he exclaims. He pauses before asking, "Does your husband know how to do any of this?"

"No," Evelyn responds blankly.

"Well if he does so happen to show up to the courts, we can hold that against him," Mr. Shaw thinks out loud. He turns to Celest and says, "Tell me when you feel better so we can walk to the car."

A few minutes go by before Celest feels ok. After she tells everyone she feels better, Mr. Shaw leads them out the back door, to the staff parking lot. He opens the doors for all the ladies before walking himself out.

Celest settles in the backseat of the car. It's a little smaller than Aunt Marie's car, and Buddy has trouble laying down because of how much he's grown. She looks out the window again. *The stars are pretty tonight.*

The police station is only five minutes away from the attorney's office. Although it is a short drive, Celest falls asleep. Evelyn gets out of the car, looking through the car window. She grins at her sleeping daughter.

Aunt Marie puts her hand on Evelyn's shoulder whispering, "She is beautiful, isn't she?"

Evelyn softly taps on the window. Buddy pipes up and stares back at her. Aunt Marie smiles at him, pointing to Celest. Buddy rubs his nose against her and lifts her head. *What is it?*

Oh. Evelyn opens the door and Celest undoes her seatbelt. As usual, Buddy hops out of the car first. Aunt Marie sticks her hand out for her to hold. Mr. Shaw waits for the family on the other side of the car.

Celest looks up at the police station. On the front of the building, there are huge letters that spell out "POLICE." The closer they get to the building, the brighter the area seems to get.

The inside of the building is no different. *Bright lights and empty space.* Mr. Shaw leads the family up to the line for the help desk. At this hour, only a few people are there, so the wait isn't very long.

The policewoman at the desk smiles at Mr. Shaw and tells him, "Long time no see. What can I help you with?" Her voice sounds a little raspy, probably from talking all day.

"I'm here to report child abandonment," he responds.

The woman spins around in her chair, reaching for a nearby file cabinet. She pulls the top drawer open and takes out a folder. Afterwards she turns to face Mr. Shaw again.

"These are the papers you'll need to fill out." The woman looks over at Celest and emphasizes, "Meet me in my office when you're done."

Mr. Shaw leads the family over to a set of empty benches. Celest hops on one of the seats and taps beside her. Buddy hops on the bench as well. Evelyn sits to the left of Celest. She leans over to her daughter asking, "Have you been writing in your diary?"

Of course I have. Celest looks up at her mother. Evelyn smiles and opens her purse. She reveals a pink diary with 'Celest' engraved on the front. "You left it at Aunt Marie's house," Evelyn explains. She hands the book over to Celest who doesn't know how to accept her gift. *Why would I need this now?* She looks at her mother with wide eyes.

Evelyn smiles advising that Celest should "Bring this with you *wherever* you go, remember?" She turns her attention back to Mr. Shaw.

Wherever I go. Mr. Shaw finishes up the paperwork and they walk to the policewoman's office. It looks much like Mr. Shaw's office, minus the family photos. The woman settles in her chair before saying anything.

Mr. Shaw hands her the paperwork. She takes it thankfully but pays little attention to it. "Where is your evidence?" she asks.

"All the evidence we need is right here," Mr. Shaw responds while pointing to the family. The officer looks at Mr. Shaw with a confused face. "They have told me that they haven't seen Ms. Evelyn's husband in five years."

The policewoman's expression turns stone cold. She picks up the phone in front of her and starts dialing a number. "I am going to call CPS," she announces.

Evelyn's eyebrows raise as she practically begs, "Are they going to take her away from us?"

Mr. Shaw looks over with concerned eyes and reassures her: "Of course not miss. We are just filing a report to them so we can track down your husband."

Mr. Shaw's comment only makes Evelyn worry more. "So, they're going to lock him up?" she frets.

He responds in a slightly confused tone, "Yes of course."

"No, no we can't do that!" Evelyn protests as she yanks the phone out of the policewoman's hands and slams it back down into its holder. The policewomen just stares at her in disbelief.

Evelyn starts quivering as she did in Mr. Shaw's office. "When he gets out, he will take it out on me! And he might take it out on her! I'm not going to let that happen!" she shouts.

Mr. Shaw and the policewoman glance at each other for a moment. "Is there something you haven't told me about your husband Mrs. Evelyn?" the policewoman asks.

Celest rolls her eyes and answers her question, "Oh yeah, I guess we never told you. He used to beat her when he was still around," she says sarcastically.

Mr. Shaw explains, "See, we've got this guy for domestic violence as well."

The police woman reassures Evelyn that everything will be ok: "As long as I'm on this case, he will never hurt you again do you understand me?"

Evelyn gives her a small nod. Losing interest, Celest looks at the diary she was given a few moments before. She takes the pen latched to the side of the book into her hands. The adults are still talking back and forth, so no one notices her. She opens to a blank page:

I am very proud of my mother for getting me this book. I am not sure what to write. I'm not sure if I even know how to write properly. After so many years not seeing my father, I enjoy that we are trying to take action against him. Even if this doesn't work out, I'm happy that we tried. My mom has gotten better, but she still doesn't stand up for herself at times. Deep down, I really want him to be put away, but I'm not going to tell anyone that. I just hope that someday father will understand what it's like to be powerless and unheard.

Celest feels a tap on her shoulder. Evelyn looks down at her with a smile: "I see you're using your diary. C'mon. It's time to go."

What do you mean it's time to go? Celest turns her attention to the police officer. In a saddened voice she asks, "Why aren't you helping us?"

The officer is taken aback by Celest's tone. Mr. Shaw quickly addresses her question, "Actually, she's helping us greatly. We are only leaving because we need to get you home."

Celest slowly turns her head in Mr. Shaw's direction.

"We need to get you in the bed so your blood sugars will be ok tomorrow," Aunt Marie says in a calm voice. The policewoman waits for Evelyn or Aunt Marie to say something else, but they never do.

Mr. Shaw and Celest's family walk to the doorway of the office. *Thank you.* Celest smiles at the policewoman before she leaves the room. *I don't remember the last time I was genuinely happy.*

"Let's go Celest," Evelyn says.

Evelyn holds out her hand. Celest's gaze stays on the officer for a few moments before she walks out the door. She takes her mother's hand and walks out of the room with her. *I will never forget you.*

Mr. Shaw drives them back to his office. *Is that it?* Once in the office, he says a few words to Evelyn and Marie, but no further action is taken. Everyone says their goodbyes to Mr. Shaw, and they return to Aunt Marie's car.

Are we actually going to get help? Celest sits in silence the whole car ride. The only thing that comforts her is the stars. *I wish my life was as bright as the stars.* Within a few moments, Celest falls asleep with Buddy resting in her lap. *Why won't it just stop?*

Chapter 4: Break Away

The sun shines through the window. Celest pops her head up. She looks to the side and sees her familiar bedside table. Home. Buddy trots to the side of the bed and does a "low" command. Celest holds her hands out in front of her face. *I feel really weak.* Her hands shake in front of her.

Buddy, not getting any praise for doing his command, starts to bark at Celest. *I can't do anything for you.* After still not receiving a treat, Buddy goes to alert another person in the house, but the door is closed. He stands on his hind legs and scratches at the door, making a lot of noise. Evelyn busts through the door, knocking Buddy back down to his feet. She looks at her daughter in the bed. Celest only gives her a blank stare back.

"Marie, I need you to grab an orange juice!" Evelyn yells out the door. She rushes up to Celest and sits her up. *I'm really tired.* Celest's eyes begin to close.

"No, no Celest," Evelyn says, "You can't go to sleep now." Before Celest has time to ask her mother why she can't sleep, Evelyn takes her PDM out of Buddy's harness and tests her.

47

Aunt Marie is in the room at this point, already instructing Celest to drink some. She looks to Evelyn and says, "We shouldn't have kept her awake so long last night. She needs proper rest, or this will happen again."

Evelyn nods and continues to keep Celest awake. Celest finds herself unable to speak anymore. *It's like I'm back in the hospital; I can only move my head.* Ten minutes pass before Celest feels any change. She still can't speak, but energy is returning to her body. A few more minutes pass and it is like nothing ever happened.

Evelyn locks eyes with Celest. "You tell me if you ever feel like this again, ok?" she instills.

Celest nods her head. Aunt Marie heads out of the room, but Evelyn stays. She sits on the bed next to Celest and starts up a conversation to distract her from her low blood sugar, "I saw you writing in your diary yesterday."

Celest looks at her mother. "I didn't know exactly what to put in there, so I wrote how I felt at the time," she robotically responds.

Evelyn reassures her that "There is no 'wrong thing' that you can put in your diary. If you ever feel down, you can write why. Maybe you want to write about your day. It's all up to you."

Celest looks over to the nightstand. Her diary is laid perfectly centered on top. "Do you think that Aunt Marie has a diary?" she somewhat randomly asks.

Evelyn thinks for a moment before honestly telling her, "I don't know. You should ask her sometime."

Maybe I should. Celest hops off of her bed and walks out the door, leaving her mother behind. Buddy follows her. From the living room she can see Aunt Marie cooking a meal for everyone. Noticing Celest, Aunt Marie looks at her and says, "Food will be ready in five minutes."

"I'm sorry," Celest replies, "but I wasn't really worried about the food. "She waits for Aunt Marie to answer, but she just continues to cook.

"I was wondering if you use a diary," Celest says seemingly to no one. She still looks like she is forcing her body to move, and she doesn't track Aunt Marie with her eyes.

Aunt Marie turns to Celest, unfazed by her weird behavior, "No, I don't use a diary."

"Then how do you cope with negative situations?" Celest asks with a sort-of confused look on her face.

"What do you mean negative situations?" Aunt Marie asks in the same sing-song tone.

Celest rationalizes, "Mom and I had to deal with my dad. I'm sure you have to deal with people too. I just wanted to know how you cope with them."

Aunt Marie's resting smile falters slightly. She looks to Celest with sadness in her eyes. "I'm sorry that you had to deal with your dad," she contemplates with herself before continuing, "I wouldn't usually tell anyone this, but I have a few different ways of coping with life."

Aunt Marie takes a moment to turn off the stove and walk over to the couch, closer to Celest. She sits down still looking concerned. "I've never been in the same situation you've been in, but I've had to deal with things myself," she motions for Celest to sit next to her, "I didn't always live here alone. I had a wonderful husband and a son who lived here with me."

Had? Aunt Marie continues, "Back then we didn't have the same medications and resources to treat a condition like yours. Unfortunately, Benji passed away from it."

Passed away? Aunt Marie stands and walks down the hallway. *Where are you going?* Buddy trots in front of Celest, following Aunt Marie. She makes a left turn, into a room Celest has never been in before. She reaches over and flips on the light.

The room is filled with every color of the rainbow. Art pieces hang from the walls, even the floor is painted with various designs. *This is amazing.*

"To answer your question again, no, I don't have a diary," She gestures to the room, "This is my diary." Aunt Marie spreads her arms out wide, showing off her works. "Take a look around."

She smiles at Celest before leaving the room. *Where do I even start?* Celest slowly makes her way around the area. Every canvas is better than the last. As she walks along, Celest realizes that all the pictures are filled with harsh colors. *Must've been angry at something.*

She continues walking with Buddy following behind her. At the end of the line of canvases, is one canvas that particularly sticks out. There's no red or black in this one. There is only blue. The canvas displays the night sky, filled with stars.

Celest turns her head towards the doorway and to her surprise, her mother stares back at her. "I see you've found my painting," Evelyn says.

Your painting? Evelyn chuckles. "Aunt Marie let me use one of her canvases. Painting is very relaxing."

No wonder it looks different than the others. "If you ever want to help me paint," Evelyn says, "You can always pop in."

Celest looks away to consider her mother's proposal. She hesitantly nods her head and walks out of the room. Even before her foot hits the exit door, she can smell Aunt Marie's cooking once again.

She makes her way down the hall to find a plate lying on the dining room table for her. Aunt Marie sits at the table, watching the living room television from afar. *I wonder what she's painting.* Celest sits down next to Aunt Marie instead of in her usual seat as to not block her view of the T.V.

Celest looks down at her plate. It's the same breakfast as always, but she sees it in a different way. *She took time out of her day to do this for me, despite her problems.* Buddy sits on the ground, wagging his tail, happy to take any food scraps that happen to fall off the table. *When I really think about it, she's been really nice to us the whole time.*

"Celest are you ok?"

She looks up from her plate. Aunt Marie stares at her with concerned eyes. *I haven't really been eating my food, have I?*

"Yes," she responds.

Aunt Marie asks, "Are you ready for your shot?"

Is anyone ever ready for these kinds of things? Celest nods her head and watches as Aunt Marie stands from her chair and walks back into Celest's room. She comes back out within a few seconds holding her PDM bag. "Don't forget to always put this back into Buddy's pouch," Aunt Marie reminds her.

She lays the small bag on the table. Celest picks it up and pricks her finger.

180

"This is so annoying," Celest says with irritation in her voice.

Aunt Marie chuckles. "Yes, it is, but you have to check your blood sugar before you eat."

Celest's familiar attitude returns as she scoffs. Aunt Marie shoots her a look before she calms down. Celest takes a quick look at what she has on her plate and turns the dial on her insulin pen. "Aren't you glad these things were invented so we don't have to use the vials anymore?" Celest comments.

Aunt Marie smiles, "It sure makes things a lot easier on you, especially at school."

I can actually manage my diabetes now, with Buddy's help of course. Celest lifts the bottom part of her shirt and sticks the needle into herself. Unlike when she was ten, the needle doesn't hurt her anymore. No more than a few seconds pass before she is zipping her bag back up, ready to eat.

Celest slots the bag into Buddy's harness who wags his tail as he looks up at her. She gives him a smile and turns her focus back to her plate. She picks up her fork and slowly eats her food. Although she is eating now, she can't help but wonder what Aunt Marie's life could've been like. *I should be writing this down.* Celest turns her body parallel to the table, getting ready to fetch her diary out of her room.

"Hey." Celest looks to Aunt Marie looking at her with a serious face. "You haven't finished your food yet," she says sternly.

Oh right. Celest hurriedly gobbles down the rest of her food. She puts her plate and silverware in the sink before darting to her room. Buddy trots along behind her.

Celest opens her bedside table to find her diary. She opens to a new page:

Aunt Marie seems so happy all the time. It's hard for me to imagine her going through a rough time. I would love to think that she has always been that way, but the scenes of her paintings suggest otherwise. She mentioned she had a family. I wonder what happened to her husband.

She closes her book. Buddy is looking up at her, wagging his tail. Celest plops herself on her bed and signals for him to sit next to her. She holds his head between both of her hands. Tears fall from her eyes. *I know I'm safe now. But I always have this feeling that he will come back.*

"Celest! It's time to go to school!" Aunt Marie calls out.

Oh right. Celest gathers herself and wipes away her tears. *I can never let them know.* Buddy hops out the bed, waiting for Celest at the door. After grabbing her bags, she follows behind Buddy, grabbing his leash from the clip next to the front door. She slowly hooks it onto him.

Aunt Marie rests her hand on Celest's shoulder. "Have a great day at school sweetie," she says with a smile.

Celest nods before opening the door. The bus is waiting outside the driveway as usual. "Bye bye," she says to Aunt Marie and her mother.

Buddy dashes out to the driveway, flinging Celest behind him. Evelyn closes the door and looks to Aunt Marie. "Are you ready to go?" she asks after Celest is out of ear shot.

***

School was bland as usual. I wish I didn't have to go because things are hard enough with dad. I still feel like he could come back. Mom is technically still married to him, so if he wanted to take me, he could. When I'm older, hopefully this will get better.

Celest looks up from her diary. She steps up to the door and knocks. No answer. She knocks again. Still no answer. *What is it now?* Celest slides her bag off of her shoulders to pull out her spare house keys. Unlocking the door, she quickly enters.

Buddy whines from the noise of the house alarm. Celest rushes over to the system's panel and disarms it. She looks over her shoulder into the kitchen. Food is left on one of the counters. *I haven't eaten since this morning.* She makes her way over to the counter and finds a note. *I hate notes.* She picks it up and reads:

Sorry if we are not home by now. We had to go down to the attorney's office. We will be back soon. -Mom and Aunt Marie

Why are they at the attorney's office? Celest holds on to the note for a few moments before finally setting it down to grab the plate of food. She sets it on the dining room table. *Dad must've come back.*

She tries to push her worries away by eating the food set in front of her. *Why couldn't they just say they were running an errand?* She feels something nudging her hand and looks down. Buddy is nudging his nose against her, trying to get her attention.

"What do you want Buddy?" Celest asks.

Buddy scoots over to Celest and rests his head on the side of her lap. *You just want me to stop stressing out, don't you?* Celest pets her dog, ignoring her food at this point. She makes her way over to the couch, setting her bag next to it. She opens up her diary once again:

I've always been afraid that he would come back and now he is. I don't know what I should do. Should I stand up to him? Will mom stand up for herself this time? Even now my whole body is trembling. I've lived through that once and I don't plan on going back anytime soon. I can't go back to being fearful all the time. And I'm older now; what if he hits me? Sometimes, I just wish I was never born so I wouldn't have to be under stress all the time.

Celest looks to the side and sees Buddy curled up next to her. She chuckles and adds an extra note:

Buddy seems to know when I'm stressed because he will lay on me. I hope he stays like that. It's nice to know that someone is there for you when you need them.

Celest stares ahead of herself. She wears her familiar frown as she tries to think of something to do. Before she can stop herself, she's back in the art room. She flips the light switch on.

The art pieces are all still there, the walls and floor still vibrant with color as well. Buddy shoves his way past

Celest and walks around the room. *I didn't know you liked art as well.* Celest walks into the room herself, looking at the art for a second time.

As long as she can remember, Celest has loved art. When she was smaller and her dad still lived with her, she would draw on pieces of paper or any napkins she happened to have laying around. She sees the world through colors, expressing herself with them. She would only draw with a pencil. Black and gray were the only colors that could describe how she felt back then. Even now, she will only draw in pencil, still fearful that someday Richard will come back.

When she looks at the paintings that Aunt Marie has made, she doesn't necessarily see the paintings as they are; she sees the colors. All the colors Aunt Marie use are harsh, just like her old sketches she made back at her old home.

She surveys the whole room before going to the one painting that stands out: her mother's. The painting hasn't changed since she first discovered it. *Mother did say I could help her with this.* Celest reaches to the right of her and picks up a paint brush. She looks over all the colors available to her, which seem to go on forever. Hovering her hand in the air for a while, she decides to put the brush down. *I don't know what I'm doing.*

Celest was never able to ask for a painting set when she was smaller. If she had the chance she would've, but her parents were too busy arguing to pay much attention to her.

She puts the brush back on the tray. She hadn't noticed before, but there are some fancy pencils on the tray as well. *Real sketching pencils! I've always wanted to use one of these!* Celest quickly grabs one of them and admires it.

She presses the pencil to the canvas. In a matter of moments, she sketches out a rough outline of a house, taking up much of the left side of the picture. She steps back to look over what she has done.

Buddy has found his way back to her, sitting in between Celest and the art utensils. He sits and watches her add to the artwork, wagging his tail. After a while he lays down, but still pays attention to Celest.

She takes a step back from the painting. *This is alright.* On top of the starry background is now a sketch of a house and trees in the distance.

"Buddy do you recognize this?" she asks her dog, knowing that she won't get an answer. "This is our old house."

Buddy looks at Celest and smiles. She reaches down and pets him while asking, "You'll never judge me, will you?"

They hear the familiar ring of the doorbell. Celest quickly puts the art supplies back as best she can without knocking anything over. *Ring!*

"I'm coming!" she shouts at the front door.

She rushes out the room, only stopping to turn off the light. *Calm down.* Buddy dances in place, excited for whoever might be on the other side of the door. Celest looks through the peephole. Evelyn and Aunt Marie patiently stand on the porch.

Celest turns the knob and smiles at her family. They greet her as they walk past. Buddy jumps up and down making Evelyn and Aunt Marie smile. "It's not like you haven't seen us before," Aunt Marie says.

They both drop their bags in the living room and sit down.

Evelyn asks Celest, "So how was school?"

It was terrible as always. "It was fine," Celest responds, not wanting anyone to worry about her.

Buddy stands next to Celest and bows. *Great.* She walks to her room and grabs a container of glucose tablets. *This has got to be one of the best inventions in the world.* She eats some of them, then walks back into the living room and gives Buddy a treat.

When she gets back, Aunt Marie and Evelyn seem to be smiling at each other. *What's going on?*

Evelyn speaks up, "We got you a surprise while you were gone."

She reaches into her purse that's lying beside her and pulls out a white rectangular box. On the front there is a picture of a device and the letters DEXCOM. *No way!* Celest rushes up to her mother. "Is this the new device I wanted?" she asks excitedly.

Evelyn nods and hands it to Celest. "I won't have to take any more finger pricks! A-And I'll be able to see my blood sugar in real time!" Celest smiles while hugging Evelyn and Aunt Marie. "Thank you so much!"

Aunt Marie asks, "Would you like us to help you put it on?"

Celest nods her head. She lets go of her family and runs to her room. She sets the box on her bed. *I wonder if this thing really works.* Celest slides the top flap of the box open, revealing the device inside. She reaches in and undoes the packaging.

She holds the new device in her hands. *This isn't right.* "Why does it look like this," she asks as she turns to her mother.

"This is how you're going to put it on," she responds, "The applicator will come off once you stick it to your body."

Celest looks back to the device, turning it in different directions. After investigating it for a few moments, she takes out its manual from the box. Evelyn, Aunt Marie, and Celest take turns reading it.

Aunt Marie says, "Pretty simple, I think! Let's try it out." Celest hands her the device attached to the applicator. "Well hold on now," Aunt Marie continues, "The manual said we need to connect this to a smartphone."

Aunt Marie calls Buddy over to her so she can take out Celest's phone from her pouch. She downloads something onto the phone and enters some of the information from the new device. Celest looks at her in curiosity but doesn't ask any questions.

Beep!

"What was that?" Celest asks.

Evelyn responds, "Don't worry. That just means it's working. Come over here so I can help you put it on the first time."

Celest walks over to her mother.

"Do you want this on your arm or your stomach?" Evelyn asks.

I always take shots in my stomach, so I assume that this won't be that different. Celest lifts her shirt for her mom. Evelyn takes the device and its applicator and sticks it to Celest's body. She looks Celest in the eyes. "Are you ready?" Celest nods.

"Ok. Three, two, one." Pop!

Ouch! Celest's body jerks off to the side. Evelyn, still having a strong grip on the applicator, accidentally rips it off the device. "Oh," she gasps, "I'm sorry!"

Celest continues to recoil with a look of horror on her face. Aunt Marie reaches out to give her a hug, but her offer is not met. Celest looks down at her stomach. The insertion site sticks to her. Evelyn takes a smaller device in her hands and puts it into the insertion site on Celest.

Aunt Marie presses some more buttons on Celest's phone. "Ok," she says, "Now we have to wait two hours for it to work." Celest whips her head to Aunt Marie. "Two hours?!" she exclaims.

Evelyn and Aunt Marie nod. *What am I going to do for two whole hours?* Seeming to be able to read her mind, Aunt Marie calls Celest to the living room. "Celest your mom and I have something we want to talk to you about," she says seriously.

Everyone leaves for the living room following Aunt Marie. Celest sits in the middle of the couch facing her family. "We've been meaning to talk to you about this for a while now," Aunt Marie prefaces.

Evelyn speaks up, "I probably should have mentioned it to you earlier, but I was afraid of what your reaction would be." Celest straightens up and rests her hand on Buddy's body. He nuzzles up close to her. Evelyn continues, "So, you know how our last names are still the same?" Celest's thoughts cut out Evelyn's voice. *How could I ever forget that I share a name with the person I hate most.* "I was thinking about getting it changed." She pauses for a second to look over at Aunt Marie. Aunt Marie gives Evelyn a reassuring glance. "But I don't only want a name change," Evelyn says, "I want to make sure he can never hurt us again."

Celest looks at her mother with a skeptical expression. "How are you going to do that?" she asks with a tinge of annoyance.

"I know you are young and don't understand the law yet," Evelyn responds. "But if mom legally separates from your father, he won't be able to touch us."

The last time we went to the "officers" they didn't help us. What makes you think they would help us now? Despite her thoughts, Celest quietly nods. Aunt Marie says, "We've actually got everything in place. We just wanted your approval first. Celest looks to the ground and asks, "You're sure that dad will never come back?"

"We promise."

Chapter 5: Someday

"You can pick anything you want."

Today is the first time I can relax. I don't have to worry about him anymore. He's not coming back. They promised. I don't know exactly what they're doing because that's for "grown folks to know," but I want to believe that it'll work out. I'm worried about mom though. She seems to still worry, and her eating habits aren't getting any better. She still doesn't have much energy to do things, though she's always been like this, so maybe that's just how she is.

It'll be my birthday soon. It's the first time I've ever gotten the chance to throw a party. I'm going to invite all my friends from school in case I won't ever get the chance again. I hope we have a great time.

Celest walks with Aunt Marie and Evelyn down the aisles of the local shop. She's supposed to be looking for a birthday present, but her freedom is enough for her. "Aunt Marie I don't know what I want," Celest admits.

She looks to Celest. "What do you mean? You can pick anything in here! I'll buy it for you!" she responds. Celest looks down. Buddy welcomes her glance, loving the attention. "I don't really know *how* to pick a birthday present. I've never done it before," Celest says blankly.

Aunt Marie gently lifts Celest's head and tells her, "It's ok. We'll walk this store as many times as you need, but we'll find you a good present." She suddenly smiles, "And this isn't even the best part! Think of all the gifts your friends will give you!"

Celest begins to walk down the isles once again. *I don't even know how a party works. I've never been to one much less thrown my own. The only parties I've ever seen are the ones on tv where they invite the whole town.*

I'm ok with the few friends I have at school. No need to invite anyone else.

While walking down one of the rows they hadn't been to before, Celest spots a flashy book. "Hey what's this?" she asks. She jogs over to the object, accidentally tugging at Buddy's leash a little too hard. She looks back at her dog who seems startled at first but goes back to smiling. "Sorry Buddy!"

She turns back to the shiny book. "Limited Edition Gold" is written on the signs surrounding it. Celest picks it up. *There's only one left.* The cover is decorated with flowers and grass, all in the same gold color. *It's beautiful.* Celest turns her head to the side. "I know what I want for my birthday!" she exclaims loud enough for the people a few rows down from her to hear.

Aunt Marie and Evelyn meet Celest next to the grand display. "Oh, that's wonderful honey!" Aunt Marie says, "You want this diary? Well, there's only one left so we better-" "No." Celest says, practically slamming the book back onto the shelf. Aunt Marie stares at her, confused for a second. Evelyn bursts out in laughter. "You were wrong about that one!" she teases while nudging Aunt Marie with her elbow.

She laughed. She actually, genuinely laughed. "I actually want my own painting set," Celest explains. Aunt Marie looks over at Evelyn, who is still trying to recover from laughing. Buddy must've thought that they were playing because he starts dancing around near Evelyn, happy as can be. "A painting set?" Aunt Marie questioned. "Yes, my very own painting set," Celest repeats while holding the book up once again. She continues, "Don't you see how pretty these flowers are on the outside of this diary? Could you imagine if I could paint these? I mean I can draw pretty well, but there are no colors in my art. I want to learn how to paint just like you!"

Aunt Marie smiles. "Well if that's what you want, that's what we'll get for you."

***

"So why do you have your own art room anyway?"

Aunt Marie freezes at the sound of this question. She looks at Celest briefly before putting on her apron. She sets all of her painting supplies up, brushing past Celest many times without saying a word. *Maybe I shouldn't have asked.*

Aunt Marie makes her way over to the first painting in the room, to the left of the door. "I wish I had a nice story to tell you about how I started painting," Aunt Marie says in a defeated tone. "But I don't. This painting here was the first one out of the bunch. I use painting as a way to cope with things. I've had a few...losses. My therapist told me that I should find something fun to do to distract myself from the pain, but I didn't know what to do at the time. I came home one day to find a small paper on the ground. I must've missed it while clearing out Benji's room. On the back there was a note written to me and a painting of me and him. So that's how I discovered painting. I haven't stopped ever since."

I never would have thought that someone so nice and seemingly happy all the time went through troubles of their own. I've always been so focused on other things that I never stopped to notice something as important as that.

Celest looks up. Aunt Marie has made her way to the other side of the room, inspecting every painting along the way, every canvas, every paper, every ounce of paint on the walls. She walks by, reliving her old memories.

She paints like I write. It's not something you do because you enjoy it for yourself, it's just something you do to keep your mind off things, to cope.

"But you..." Aunt Marie says out of the blue, "You and your mother have something special here." They both gaze at the unfinished painting. "My very last canvas. It's going to be beautiful. I already think it's beautiful and it's not even finished! It's definitely better than anything I've ever made." Aunt Marie turns back to her paintings as quickly as she turns away from them. "Maybe someday I'll find it in me to paint something like that," she finally says.

"Knock, knock," Evelyn chimes, peering her head into the entrance of the room. Aunt Marie smiles. "We were just talking about you."

Celest looks at her mother standing in the doorway. *You seem happy now. I hope you can stay that way for a long time.* Evelyn walks towards Celest and Aunt Marie, looking over the paintings in the room again. *You seem like you're happy, but your condition seems the same. I wish you would eat more.*

"Oh, Celest did you want to do something else with that painting?" Evelyn asks.

Celest snaps out of her daze and looks over her shoulder at the painting of the house. "Sure," she responds weakly.

Evelyn walks to the paintbrushes and other supplies. She hovers her hand over a few things before picking out what she will use. Celest isn't focused on the painting at all anymore. She can only see her mother's trembling hands and her tiny wrists. *Why don't you get better?*

Celest tries to shake away her thoughts, but they won't give. She makes a comment to distract herself: "You did a really good job on the house I outlined mom." Evelyn smiles and responds, "I honestly wish I found out this talent before. So, what should we do next?"

Celest studies the house again. *This is supposed to represent our old house, not this one. We're still connected to it. I've strayed away, but I'm afraid that you might not ever be able to. Why can't I help you mom?*

Celest picks up a pencil from the art tray. She quickly draws out an outline resting on the roof of the house. She begins to talk as she adds details to the figure. "My name has to do with the stars. You're supposed to only get good things from the stars. You are supposed to wish on the stars. You are supposed to hope on the stars," Celest pauses as her eyes well up with tears, "But I fear that one day I will only have the stars. And no matter how much I wish, my dream will never come true."

Celest steps back to admire her drawing for a moment. "Mom, I don't want you to go." Evelyn looks into Celest's eyes which are now bursting with tears. She holds her arms out and pulls her daughter close to her. "I'm not going anywhere honey," she says softly.

Celest holds onto her mom for a long time. *Why are you lying to me? I know you're not well. Just tell me the truth.* Evelyn interrupts, "Go and wipe your tears. You can watch me paint when you come back." Celest begrudgingly pulls away from her mother and walks out the room, head hung low.

"I'm sorry I failed you," Aunt Marie says with a weary voice.

Evelyn chuckles. "Oh, you didn't fail anyone. You've done nothing but help. If anything, I failed her. I was so focused on my suffering I didn't even think that my pain affected her."

Evelyn lifts her hand and starts painting over Celest's new sketches. She says to their painting, "One day you'll look at the stars and I'll be looking right back at you."

Chapter 6: Aren't They Beautiful?

"Come on mom!"

Today I suggested that we should go on a walk. When is the last time we have even been outside? I brought my notebook around with me just in case I see something pretty or want to write something down. Aunt Marie is staying at home to rest, but we are bringing Buddy with us. Today will be a good day.

"Hold on Celest. I have to put my walking shoes on," Evelyn says.

Celest waits by the door. She's wearing a blue top and white shorts, her favorite outfit. Buddy sits next to her, wagging his tail at the thought of going outside. *You're really excited, aren't you?* Buddy looks up at her, smiling away. Celest's things are sitting snug inside of his harness.

Evelyn emerges from down the hallway. "Ready to go honey?" Celest nods and smiles. "What about you?" she asks while looking down at Buddy. He turns his head back to her and continues to smile. "I'll take that as a yes."

Evelyn reaches behind Celest to open the front door. Buddy bolts out the door, dragging Celest behind him. Evelyn chuckles and follows them, making sure to close and lock the door behind her. She shouts, "Hey, wait for me!" as she tries to catch up to Celest and Buddy speeding down the driveway.

"I brought my new journal with me today," Celest tells her mother when she finally catches up. Panting, she responds, "That's great honey! Have you been using it at all?"

Celest shows a huge smile. "Yes of course I've been using it! I even wrote something in there while I was waiting for you at the door!" Evelyn returns her daughter's smile. "Can I see?" she wonders.

Can she see? I never thought about anyone looking in my journal, especially not her. What if she sees the things I wrote about her?

Celest struggles to let out an answer. "I-it's my journal. I don't w-want you to see w-what's in t-there," she clunkily responds.

Evelyn's expression quickly changes. Her eyes widen, and her mouth stands agape. "Sorry," she says, "I should've thought about that before." She turns her gaze off of Celest and to the nature around them.

Celest shies away from her mother ever so slightly.

I hope that didn't sound too suspicious...

They continue to walk a little ways before reaching the end of their street. The asphalt ahead of them slowly turns into gravel. Evelyn looks back to Celest's journal resting in her daughter's hands. "I want you to take this wherever you go," she says while pointing at the book. "I want you to write all of your thoughts in it every day."

What a strange thing to keep telling me. Has she not said that a hundred times before? Celest gives Evelyn a slight nod. They can't see any of the houses anymore; the only thing that surrounds them is mother nature and the sounds she makes. Celest takes a deep breath, loving the scent of the forest trees. Various animals are heard scampering around and passing them by in the bushes. She sets her eyes on a group of deer who have gathered to drink around a pond.

Evelyn takes out her own notebook and begins writing in it. Her hand moves across the page like she's written all her life, which she probably has. She doesn't look up until she is finished writing down all of her thoughts, and even then, she's still in her own world.

By the time Evelyn finishes writing, Celest and Buddy have perched on a rock near the pond. Buddy carefully watches the deer happily skipping around and playing with each other. Celest is too busy writing in her own book to notice anything else.

Today mom and I are going on a walk to the nearby trail in the woods. I still don't think she is well, even after all that's happened. I think she is hiding something from me. She knows that we aren't exactly comfortable with each other, but she insisted that we take this walk today.

I know I have written in here time and time again that she is fragile and needs to do better, but that doesn't mean I don't love her. I see how thin she is and how little she eats. Aunt Marie tries to hide it, but I can still see it. Mom isn't well and she hasn't been for a long time.

Celest looks out in front of her after writing that last word. *I know that you're not ok. Why won't you tell me what's wrong?* Buddy nuzzles his head a little closer to her and whines. Celest looks down at him and he stares back with seemingly sad eyes. Celest still hasn't figured out how he always knows what she is thinking, but in this moment, she can only be thankful for him. Who else would she be able to share her troubles with?

Celest feels something on her shoulder. She whips her head back to find her mom standing behind the rock she is resting on. Evelyn has her hand resting on Celest and is peering over her shoulder. Celest quickly slams her book shut in fear of her mother seeing what she has written, but it's in vain.

"Celest," Evelyn says in a low tone. "I wanted to come here with you to show you how beautiful the world can be." Celest looks up at her mother in confusion. Evelyn responds by pointing to the deer that were sipping from the lake a few minutes ago. "You see them? They're beautiful, right?" Celest looks over to the animals in silence. "I realize that we don't have many happy memories together, do we? I thought it would be nice to show you that there is beauty in the world just like you."

Buddy perks up and lunges at Evelyn. He jumps up at her and licks all over her face. Celest laughs. "I think Buddy's trying to tell you something," she says while smiling at her mom. "And what is that?" Evelyn responds. Celest perks up: "He's telling you that you're beautiful too."

Celest looks back at the lake and waves one final goodbye to the animals before hopping off the rock. She doesn't say anymore to her mother, or Buddy for that matter, and walks right past them. *It's time to go home.* "Wait!" Evelyn calls after her daughter. Celest turns her head, stopping for a moment. "Don't you want to stay a little longer? It's only been thirty minutes." Celest doesn't answer, she just turns away and keeps walking.

Buddy stops playing with Evelyn and trots to keep up with Celest. Evelyn, however, doesn't follow behind them. She slowly approaches the lake. Looking at her reflection through the water, she runs her hand through the warm pond. "One day," she says, "I'll be back to visit you. I hope by then you can forgive me."

She collapses to her knees, unable to hold back her emotions anymore. Tears stream down her face. All the tears she had ever held back, are flooding out of her now. She's tired. A person can only take so much. And when it's too much, like a piece of glass, they shatter.

***

You're going to be ok.

You're going to be ok.

You are ok.

You...

You're...

You're not ok...

Shattered is not the right word for how Celest is feeling right now; obliterated might start to describe what she's feeling. She can't believe what she's looking at. Her mom is cooped up in a hospital bed just like she was years ago. She had made the walk back to Aunt Marie's house and assumed her mom was just a little ways behind her, but she was wrong.

After ten minutes of not seeing Evelyn coming through the door, Aunt Marie went looking for her. Evelyn had stayed at the pond. Her body couldn't take it anymore; she was under too much pressure. Holding in all that pain for so many years finally caught up with her. *I knew something was wrong. Why didn't you tell me what was wrong?*

Evelyn clenches Aunt Marie's hand, now laying in the hospital bed. "I'm sorry," Evelyn says weakly. Aunt Marie doesn't respond at first, she just strokes the top of her head whispering, "It's ok. You did the best you could."

Buddy whines from the opposite side of the room. *I know.* Celest decides to stand from her chair and walk over to her mother, so Buddy can be with her. He drags his feet one after the other, tail between his legs, unlike his usual trot. He rests his head on the edge of the bed, level with

Evelyn's body. Celest strangely doesn't cry at this sad sight. *She'll be fine.*

A couple doctors enter the room from the hospital hall. Everyone turns to look at them, hoping for good news. One of the doctors lock eyes with Aunt Marie and secretly signals her to remove Celest from the room. She nods before turning to Celest.

"Come on honey. We can go and get something to eat on the way out," she assures.

I saw that...

Celest slowly pans her head in the direction of the doctors and gives them a sad smile. She holds her hand out flat behind her and waves Buddy over. Buddy looks at Celest, but then rests his head back down on Evelyn's body. Aunt Marie gently grabs Celest's hand to lead her to the open doorway of the hospital room. She obeys Aunt Marie until she steps one foot out the door. "Celest what's going on? What happened?" Aunt Marie asks.

Celest keeps staring forward, eyes wide, looking into nothing. Aunt Marie bends down in front of her and tries to meet her eyes, but Celest keeps staring at that one spot. "Celes-"

"Stop. Please just stop" is the only response Aunt Marie gets. Celest's voice has gone cold: "I know that you want to protect me, but you just make me feel confined in my own body. I'm smarter than you think." Celest pauses and takes a deep sigh. She pivots her body to face her mom. "I know that I don't say it often, but I really love you mom. I love you so much. Even when I gave you a hard time when I was younger, and I still do now, I see that you really tried. I see that you really *wanted* to be the mother that I needed. I saw you struggle, and I saw you in pain most days. But I also saw how much you loved me and how hard you tried to show me. I'm sorry for being so mischievous and often causing trouble. The painting we made together was the best thing that's ever happened to me. I loved being with you and enjoying our time with no worries for once. But I have to go now..."

Celest looks over her mom one last time before walking out of the room. Aunt Marie can only stare with her mouth wide open. "She's a smart kid," one of the doctors says, "Take good care of her." Buddy shakily moves from his spot, tail still tucked, and ears still drooped. He meets Aunt Marie at the other side of the room. He gives her a small nudge on the legs before walking out of the room as a way of saying "It's time to go."

Aunt Marie gives a look to the doctors who let her know it is ok to leave. She walks out of the room, leaving Evelyn behind. She hangs her head low on the way to the hospital's parking lot. Celest doesn't say anything either, instead she is writing away in her little notebook.

Counting the days you are here with me,

We didn't have many shared

But there were a few

I spent with you

That made me feel loved

Though I wish you loved you

As much as I love you

And cared for yourself

The way that I do.

I knew it. I knew that this would happen. I knew it. I knew it. I knew it. I could have stopped it. I should have tried harder. I should've done more. I should've.... I *should've....But I can't...And I never will. I am doomed here, a failure. Just like dad has told me so many times. He was right. He was right. He was right about me. I can't believe he was right about me. I am nothing. I could never be anything. I should have never been here. I was a mere mistake. I should have never tried to be anything. He was right. He was right...I knew it.*

Celest notices the pages in front of her dotted with wet spots. She looks up, tears streaming down her face. *Why was I such a bad daughter?* She continues to walk through the endless rows of cars, looking for a way to escape, escape this horrible reality that she is trapped in. *So many families here for similar reasons. How many of these cars will drive away today with less passengers than it came? How many people are feeling the same way I am? How many times will someone get hurt here? There's more than just me, right? Or am I alone again, like I always am? Am I the only one who has such a terrible life that the only person that I can hold on to leaves me too? Does anyone else have to suffer like this? Does-*

A voice cuts Celest's line of thought: "Tears are the way we communicate when we can not speak." Aunt Marie looks down at her and continues, "But never think tears are for the weak. That's what my mother used to tell me." *Why are you speaking to me?* Celest keeps her eyes down, refusing to acknowledge Aunt Marie. *Who do you think you are?* She forces herself to suppress her feelings, pushing her tears back farther and farther until finally they stop; she stops. *It is better for me to have no emotion than to show them and get manipulated. I won't let you get to me.*

I'll never let anyone get to me ever again.

Chapter 7: To the Moon

12 days

4 hours

37 minutes

That's how long you've been in there for. Who knows how much longer till you get out. I hear that you're doing alright. You're eating and drinking just fine, and you can sleep through the night well, but that's not exactly extraordinary. I understand some people want to be positive, but I prefer not lying to myself. Just tell me if my mom will make it through this or not. Don't feed me with the 'everything will be ok' lie just to 'keep me from worrying.' I never understood that. How could I not worry? Why won't anyone just tell me the truth?

Aunt Marie took me to visit mom again today; it was our 11th visit. I still don't know why Aunt Marie wouldn't let us visit one day. I'm sure she had her reasons.

"Breakfast is ready!" Celest hears from somewhere in the house. *Oh yeah...It's morning...* "Coming," she responds. *Did I sleep last night?* Celest slowly glances around her room. *Something's off.* Ignoring this feeling for the time being, she stands and stretches. Slowly she makes her way out of her room and into the kitchen.

Aunt Marie stands near the dining room table. With a quick glance Celest can see that there's no food in sight. *What trick is she pulling today?*

"I know this is different," Aunt Marie starts, "but I thought both of us could use a breather." Aunt Marie awkwardly shuffles past Celest, like a singer with stage fright. She clears her throat, "How about we paint something? I know you enjoy art sometimes. It could be nice to let go for a while, right?" *You're acting strange...*

Celest mindlessly follows Aunt Marie to her canvas room. She flips the lights on to find that most of Aunt Marie's paintings are pushed up against the right wall. She gives a confused look to Aunt Marie but the avid painter only stares to the center of the room. Turning her attention back to the interior, Celest sees the painting her and her mom had been working on. *When did this happen?*

Standing in front of Celest was a finished piece, complete with Evelyn's signature at the bottom. Replacing her sketch marks are elegant strokes of paint and detail. She could see everything: the way the wind seemed to sway the tree leaves, the weathered wood of the house, the contrast of the sky and the stars, the moonlight shining onto the figure resting on top of her cage, and finally, she could see the girl on top, eyes shining as bright as the stars.

Celest stares at their creation with tears inside her eyes. As desperate as she is to lock her emotions away, to never cry in front of anyone again, she can't keep her own promise. In the spotlight of her mother, Celest will always care. Despite spending all her years longing for a mom that turned out differently, she can't suppress her tears for her. Evelyn tried the best she thought she could. That eats Celest up every day. *She thought she was doing well. She thought this was the right way. And all I did was scoff.*

Once the first tear falls, I can't even feel the rest. Aunt Marie doesn't bother Celest. She pulls some new brushes, paints, and canvases out of a few drawers. After a few moments she rearranges her items to have two propped up canvases in the newfound empty space of the room. Quietly she brings a stool to each canvas and claims one as her own. She sets her paints up the way that she likes, all next to her on a separate surface. After looking over her paints for a while, she nods her head like she already knows what her new painting will look like. During that brief planning period, she dips a brush in the paint and begins her craft.

Aunt Marie's hands glide over the canvas like water. Every stroke seems calculated, yet elegant; she's in her element. "You know Celest," she says without breaking, "You're only the second case of Type 1 I've ever had."

Now that's something interesting. Celest breaks her intense stare and looks towards the voice she hears.

She sees Aunt Marie sitting in front of her canvas and the canvas she set up next to her. She walks over to the empty stool and sits.

Aunt Marie clarifies, "I had one other case a several years before you came in; a *little boy*."

Aunt Marie pauses her hand, paint sitting still. *A little boy?* "First you must understand that your condition was not researched when this boy came in. He was only ten years ahead of you, but we did not have the technology to treat T1D like we do now. Everything was experimental; life expectancies weren't long, things of that nature."

Celest notices how Aunt Marie doesn't have the strong gaze she usually holds. She's not looking at Celest at all. She's fixated on the incomplete canvas in front of her, just as Celest is tranced by her mother's painting. *She must be lost in her memories.*

"I was much younger than I am now," Aunt Marie continues, gliding her brush across her canvas, "and I didn't know much of anything about the disease. This was before I received my medical license." *How did you treat someone then? No, pay attention.* "It was pretty late at night and the boy had already been asleep. The boy's father was in the living room reading as he usually did on the weekends. He didn't think of anything but the words flying across the pages of his book. The father began to hear a light tapping from somewhere in the house, but he chose to ignore it; it could've been the trees outside..." *This is very oddly specific for a patient...*

    Aunt Marie turns her gaze to Celest almost to check if she's still there. Once she's satisfied, she picks up, "The knocking continued lightly in the background for a while...until it stopped. The father got curious for a moment but didn't have time to sit on it. A huge thud, like a barbell had been dropped, hit his ears. His curiosity turned to worry as he rushed down the hall towards the noise. His heart sank as his feet carried him to the foot of his son's room. There he saw his son face-down on the floor. The boy wasn't responding to anything the father tried..." Aunt Marie pauses, "I was the one who rushed the boy to the hospital, as helpless and clueless as I was. When we got there, they didn't understand what was wrong with him. They ran test after test, but nothing ever came up. He was in a coma. Finally, someone tested his blood sugar off a whim. The meter couldn't even register how high the boy's blood sugar was."

Aunt Marie suddenly drops her paintbrush. With a shaky voice she speaks, each one of her words angrier than the last: "They told me that there was nothing they could do for Benji, that he had a rare condition and there was no way to get him out of the coma. I became a doctor in spite. I was angry. Why wasn't there a way to save my son? What research wasn't done yet? Why wasn't there another way? So, I devoted my life to diabetic research. You are proof that I haven't done this in vain."

She's gone this entire time carrying this on her shoulders. That's why she wanted to help us. It's not some elaborate set up. She genuinely wants to help us. Or...that's what she wants me to think and I'm letting another person get to me, yet again...Stop. I have to stop trusting people so easily. But maybe she's telling the truth?

"Oh," is the only thing that comes out of Celest's mouth. She had too many thoughts, too many passing waves of emotions. She sits in front of her designated canvas. *Benji...*

That could've been me...

Celest feels her mouth stiffen, almost like it has been glued shut. The aura radiating throughout the room is heavy, with a hint of familiarity. Aunt Marie and Celest paint in this realm for a while. *It's nice to sit silently sometimes. It's easier for people to hear you in silence. Time feels stopped but quick simultaneously. Nothing else matters but the silence.* Time continues to pass nonetheless and soon the artists' hands stop.

"It's time to go," Aunt Marie says in a raspy tone.

"Wher-" Celest starts but is quickly cut off.

Aunt Marie slowly stands, stretching her knees, "Time to see your mother."

Why now? Celest tucks away her confusion for now. She forces her legs to lift her off the floor and walk her to the doorway. *Something is wrong...Or maybe it's just anxiety...?* Celest stands in the middle of the room, not moving for a while. *No, no. She's never done this before. Why now?* Not noticing her fallen head at first, she looks up. The lights are shut off. *Has it been that long?*

Celest shakes her head. *It's all in my head. Nothing is wrong. Everything is fine. Just like usual. Am I fine usually?* A loud noise interrupts Celest's thought. Her head whips over to see that a paint canister has fallen over. *Great.* She rolls her eyes as she walks to the small puddle on the floor. *Not too much spilled.* She pays the paint no mind. Just as quickly as the canister fall, it is returned to its shelf and the paint is wiped up. *Just another inconvenience...nothing new.*

She turns to leave but is stopped when she sees something peculiar. Her painting is faintly glowing in the darkness of the room. It's just bright enough to notice. *I must be losing it.* Celest calls her trusted dog to her, who she had largely not thought about for the whole day. Buddy rises from a small dog bed in the corner of the room. *Were you just going to sit there in the dark?* He looks at his owner and smiles. *Nothing is wrong with me. Are you sure?* As if reading her mind, Buddy walks ahead of her and sits in the doorway, his silhouette peering back at Celest. Buddy's darker clone seemed to be watching over her ominously.

Celest's eyes wander back to the painting which still faintly glows. Only the girl and the stars seem to have this effect in the painting. *Weird.* She reaches out and drags her fingers along the girl's body, feeling the smoothness of the paint. She wears a stoic but thoughtful expression. "What are you trying to tell me...?" she faintly whispers.

"Do you see it?" a voice asks.

Huh?

"Let's go," it finishes.

Celest slowly turns her head, "Ok Aunt Ma-"

No one is there.

Hello?

***

The car ride to the hospital is oddly quiet. Celest's mind is full, but it's fuzzy. *Something is off.* Aunt Marie has her usual music playing on the radio: slightly outdated pop music. Songs that must've come from when she was in her prime. Buddy is somewhere in the car, though if Celest was asked on his whereabouts, she would likely not have an answer.

I feel off. Someone is missing. And somebody was trying to tell me something. What if it was a warning? What am I not understanding? What is it? Why do I not understand? WHY DON'T I UNDERSTAND? What is happening? Why are you speaking to me now? What did I do? What is going to happen? I can't think. I'm overthinking. It's nothing. Everything is fine. I'm fine. It'll pass. It has to.

"Could you please turn off that annoying music!" Celest suddenly yells.

Aunt Marie nearly slams on the brakes. "What is wrong with you?!" she retaliates.

"I'm sorry. I just...I don't know..." Celest mumbles out.

Aunt Marie opens her mouth but doesn't say anything. She looks at Celest with a sense of familiarity, but as much as Celest peeks at Aunt Marie from the corner of her eyes, she can't figure out why she looks at her that way. Aunt Marie readjusts her hands on the steering wheel and takes a deep breath. Her eyes mindlessly track the road. *I'm sorry.*

Celest lifts her head but can't bring herself to look at Aunt Marie directly. *I always manage to mess things up. All I do is hurt people.* She instead lulls her head over to Buddy who is sitting in the back seat. *At least I can't hurt you.* She reaches out and gives him a pat on his head, pausing for a moment to take a good look at him. *Always smiling...always happy. Must be nice.*

Celest retracts her hand and forcefully pushes her back into her seat. She looks straight ahead, fiddling with her hands. She picks under her fingernails anxiously. Her mind is fuzzy, and she can't think of anything but her mother. During their visits, she has found herself in this state often. The guilt of how she treated her mother in the past is eating away at her in some way. *Why did I say that? Why did I think that way? Why didn't I do that better?* It's an interesting feeling. The pit in the bottom of her stomach only grows larger, but there was no way to fix it. She put herself here. She will have to figure it out on her own. *If only I did a better job. If only I was kinder. If only dad never existed. If only I was better. If only I was a better dau-*

"We're here."

What? Celest slowly turns her head to her left, her eyes unnaturally wide, like she had seen something she shouldn't have. Aunt Marie's voice almost sounded like a whisper. Celest trails her eyes to Aunt Marie's hand which is outreached to hers. *How could I not notice that?* Celest pans her sight through all the windows. *We are actually here.*

"I don't think she wants to see me today," Celest mutters.

"What makes you think that?" Aunt Marie responds in a very soft tone. Celest has always admired how sympathetic she could be. She always wants to make everyone around her feel at ease. It's one of the things that makes her a good doctor.

"Uhm...I just..." Celest stutters. "I think I saw something earlier. It seemed like something I was supposed to know the meaning of, but I didn't. It could've been her talking to me."

Aunt Marie pauses a moment before she speaks. "Celest, sometimes we aren't meant to understand the messages sent to us. Sometimes we are meant to grow older and look back on those messages for their true meanings. I think that whatever message has been sent to you might be a lesson for later."

Celest doesn't have a particular reaction to what Aunt Marie says. She just sits there. *She's such a mysterious woman. She just knows.* She doesn't dwell on her thoughts for too long. She simply opens the door and steps out of the car. *She just knows.* She hears the soft closing of the opposite door and then another door opens and closes once again. It is time for them to make their way inside, yet Celest stays glued to the concrete. *It's just a normal visit. This is how it's always been.* But the truth is that today is different. She couldn't answer why. It is just *different.*

Celest manages to walk to the other side of the car, to where Buddy and Aunt Marie are. Everything from there is a blur. *What was it trying to tell me? What was she trying to tell me? What have I missed? What haven't I done? What is the point of this? Why now? What am I missing? Where did I go wrong? Did I go wrong? Are you trying to prevent me from going wrong? Are you trying to help me at all? Am I going crazy? Was I hallucinating? Is It all my fault? What is my fault? What have I done? Have I done anything? Maybe I should take a breather. Maybe I shouldn't. What do you want me to do? Do you exist? Do I? Who am I trying to talk to? Can they hear me? Does anyone ever hear me? I need to see her today. Today is important. Why is today important? Why won't you tell me? What is wrong with me? Is there anything wrong with me? Didn't I say that before? What am I-*

"This way please ma'am"

Huh?

There Celest is, standing in the hospital corridor.

When did I-

"Thank you very much"

Who is-

Before Celest has a chance to register what's going on, Aunt Marie pulls her to the side of her mom's hospital bed. She looks down at her mother with a blank stare. Evelyn's eyes are closed, and her chest moves steadily up and down as she is sleeping. Celest watches the several monitors and tubes hooked up to her mother. They are holding on to Evelyn, just as Celest wishes she would've held on to her too.

Aunt Marie and Evelyn's nurse talk in a corner of the room. *Medical stuff I assume.* They seem to be having light conversation, but Aunt Marie's eyebrows are downturned like she is receiving some important information. She occasionally glances over to Celest and her mom. Her arms are folded, and it doesn't look like they will be done with their conversation any time soon.

Celest returns her gaze to her sleeping mother. She leans her face close to Evelyn's left ear and softly asks, "What were you trying to tell me earlier?" Evelyn doesn't respond. "I know it was you in the art room. You're always talking about spirit and faith. I know it was you. What were you trying to say?"

Evelyn remains sleeping. The corners of her lips rest in a small upturn. *It is still weird to see you smile.* Celest takes this time to examine the rest of her mother's face. She mostly looks the same as she was when she was healthy. Well, maybe not healthy, just when she was out of the hospital. *I don't think I've ever really seen your body in good condition...but you not having so much of a change must be a good thing, right?* The bags under Evelyn's eyes are still present even in her peaceful state. Her cheekbones are still a little too defined, but Celest doesn't think anything of them. It's how she always is. Surely, she will get better with time.

Celest listens to the sound of Evelyn's heart monitor. Her heart beats steadily and rhythmically. *Funny how a heart that's gone through so much, can still beat so strong.* She finds a sort of comfort in hearing the beeps of the machine and watching its green line rise and fall. It is predictable. The beeps are always steady. *One after the other, like the ticking of a clock. You always know that it'll keep going.* She decides to take a seat and continues to think to herself. She settles in, wondering about miscellaneous things.

Some time passes, and Aunt Marie gestures to the doorway. The nurse turns around to see a doctor entering. They exchange a greeting, and the nurse catches the doctor up on Evelyn's state and how she had been doing over the past few hours. They smile at each other, speaking light heartedly. Aunt Marie joins in on the conversation, wanting to know the details of Evelyn's condition. The three of them spoke briefly after their initial conversation about the general state of the hospital before the doctor made their way over to Evelyn's bed. They check the monitors and make sure Evelyn's vitals are in range.

The nurse meets the doctor on the other side of the bed. "It's time for her to eat again," she says in a sweet voice. The nurse gently places her hand on Evelyn's shoulder and says her name softly. She continues to say her name, as she didn't respond the first time. They wait patiently for Evelyn to notice.

The doctor looks at the nurse in concern after Evelyn still doesn't respond. They quicky look over the monitors hooked to her, but they haven't seemed to change. The nurse shares a concerned expression. As if communicating telepathically, the nurse and doctor split off, the nurse turning to Celest, and the doctor beginning to tinker with Evelyn's tubes.

"Excuse me, could you go over with Dr. Marie please," she asks Celest.

Why? Celest looks at the nurse for a second, being broken from her trance. She thinks about refusing, but she sees the nurse's serious expression. "Uhh, sure," she responds.

Celest stands and makes her way to Aunt Marie. *So, I can't sit there now?* Aunt Marie grabs hold of Celest's hand and looks to the nurse. The nurse looks back at Aunt Marie with a different expression, one Celest had never seen before.

"Why is she l-"

"Let's go," Aunt Marie interrupts.

"But we haven't even finished-"

"Let's go," she demands.

Aunt Marie begins to walk towards the doorway, ignoring Celest's objections. *What has gotten into you?* Celest tries to pull back but is only met with more force. They are nearing the doorway when Celest hears a change in the environment: the beeps have stopped. She couldn't hear the clicking of her mother's clock any longer. Everything seems to slow down around her. *What is happening!?*

Celest feels like she is useless in this moment, only able to catch a glimpse of what is happening before she is pulled away. But she sees enough. She sees Evelyn's jolt as she gasped for air. She sees the nurse and the doctor rush over to her. She sees the horde of doctors and nurses rush into the room behind her. She sees how Aunt Marie does her best to shield her from what is happening, but it is too late. She hears Evelyn begin to flatline. He hears the panic in everyone's voices.

I can't hear her heart. The comfort that I had been listening to all this time is gone. This is what I was warned about. She tried to tell me. I can't hear her heart. I was right there with her. All I had to do was wake her up. Why didn't I wake her up? I can't hear her heart. You can't leave me. I have no one. I can't hear her heart.

I can't feel my heart...

Chapter 8: New Beginnings

    I don't know what to do. You've always told me to write in this book so I'm trying to do it more. Aunt Marie is taking care of me now. She's doing a decent job, but I don't let her know that. Besides her I have no one. I live my life away from everyone else. Well, I don't really live...I exist away from everyone else. She makes me meals three times a day, but I think she is starting to notice how full my plate is after I finish "eating." She trusts me to be home alone sometimes. I think she doesn't really have a choice because of her hours in the hospital, but freedom is freedom. She wanted me to help her look through your things, but I couldn't. As much time as I *spent violating your respect, I figured that I could do this one thing for you. I've noticed that your notebook is still on your nightstand, but I've never opened it. To be honest, I'm afraid of what I'll find. You didn't speak much, but I now understand that people can write a whole lot more than they outwardly share. I do wish that I would've given you the opportunity to share those thoughts with me. For now, I don't deserve to know what they were. I miss you every day and would love to be with you again.*

Celest closes her book. She goes through her days, one second at a time. She sits in her room and thinks all day about her mother, wondering why this had to happen to her. Occasionally, she sits with Buddy. Even he seems slightly sadder, his smile not quite as big as it used to be, but he still sticks by Celest every second of every day.

Celest looks down at her dog. He returns her gaze and slowly wags his tail. Some things never change. *Are you going to leave me too?* She walks to her room to pick up Buddy's harness. *Let's go.* Celest attaches Buddy to his leash. Buddy excitedly leads Celest to the door. He takes her down the same path that they walked with Evelyn. Celest is carried through the neighborhood effortlessly, almost like she is floating on the clouds. The houses blur into unrecognizable shapes and colors. She doesn't really notice anything around her. The kids outside devolve into bodyless voices, cast into the wind. The animals who stray in the woods fade into the brush. Her own body becomes part of the background. She knows she exists, but that's it. There is nothing that sticks out about her. Anything and everything is more important.

Celest is stopped by something bumping into her shins. She looks down and sees Buddy sitting next to the pond. He's right next to the rock that they've stopped at every day now. Celest finds herself sitting on it and facing the water. She doesn't recall exactly how she got there, but she pays it no mind. *I am here now.* She takes a deep breath and resonates with the sounds of nature. *There is nothing. It's only me. And even then, that is nothing.*

She continues to sit there without a real goal. She's given up on those useless things. There's no point in having goals if...Well the way she puts it, *why have goals when you don't have enough time to reach them?* Goals take time and *I don't have much of that anyway. If mother were here, she would tell me to push on, but...It's not important.*

Celest absently pulls out her notebook. She unhooks the pencil from inside and allows the words to be written.

Aunt Marie says that she spotted a girl around my age that walks her dog along this path. I'm not sure why she mentioned this to me, but I assume it's her way of trying to help me. It won't. I know she's just trying to help and that I should listen to her, but I just can't. I don't care enough to pay attention to that girl or any other for that matter. My life is no longer my own. Life has sent me crashing tidal waves and I just let it do its thing now. Whichever way the tide pulls me I'll go. There is no point in fighting anymore. This girl lives across the way from us. Aunt Marie says their family moved in not too long ago. I think that's strange though because shouldn't I have noticed her walking as well? Anyways, she probably wants me to introduce myself. I don't want to interact with any more people than I need to, but I don't really have anything else to do. She won't like me anyways, so it'll be a quick interaction. I'll figure it out when I run into her.

Celest closes her book. She traces her fingers over the spine, remembering how her old one felt. She has gone through several notebooks since her mother gifted her one, but she keeps them all on her bookshelf. The one she is using now is made of leather which is different from the hard books she is used to holding. This won't be the last leather notebook she owns. She has many more years to go.

Buddy takes this time to look around. He spots his old friends: the deer. One of them walks up to him and nudges his nose. Buddy smiles and entertains the animal for some time. Celest notices and steals a glance at both of them. *Cute.* Her fondness doesn't last too long though. Memories and feelings seem to leave her nowadays. *I just want to be happy.* They sit for a little while, greeting the various animals that pass by. Squirrels, bunnies, and foxes are among the bunch. Celest tracks every single one that comes into sight until they vanish. This gets old after a while, so they set off on their path again.

On their way out of the woods, Celest notices a figure walking a bit ahead of her. The person isn't very pronounced, but they are around the same height as her and are wearing an all-black hoodie. Looking a few feet in front of them, she sees a white blur bouncing along with them. *That must be that girl I was talking about. What luck...* Celest rolls her eyes to herself for writing about this girl in her book earlier. *Well, I promised...*

Celest picks up her pace. *What am I doing? How do I even greet her? When's the last time I introduced myself to someone?* She continues to ponder while keeping her eyes on her target. *Is this weird? Should I wait for another time?* The closer she gets to the girl, the more lopsided and awkward her steps become. *I don't know what I'm doing.*

Celest momentarily takes her mind off how she is going to greet this person, and instead observes her more. She's close enough to recognize that the girl has a long white pair of earbuds in her ears. The wires fall down her body into her hoodie pocket. The leash she uses on her dog is black and grey much like the rest of her outfit. *Interesting style.* Nothing else really stands out about her that Celest can see. *Predictable.*

She'll notice if I walk next to her. Celest allows her thoughts to control her, as she matches the speed of this girl. Celest doesn't say anything to her but gets close enough to her for her to notice. The girl doesn't have a big reaction like she predicted. Instead, the girl just shifts over a few feet away from her. *Hello?* Celest shuffles in the same direction to restore the close distance between them.

The girl turns her head to look at Celest and abruptly stops walking. Celest mimics her. *I must seem like the weirdest person right now...* The girl seems to read Celest's mind and sharpens her glare.

"Can I help you?" she asks with uncertainty staining her voice.

Ah what to say, what to say! "Um..." Celest pauses for a moment, distracted by the girl's beautiful elegance shining through. The girl's eyes are a deep brown, reminding Celest of her mother. Her eyelids don't quite stay open all the way, and her stare is just slightly off. *Just like mom...* This familiarity, though fleeting, makes Celest smile. *If only I could've smiled with you...*

Celest's smile reaches her eyes when she says, "Sorry to bother you I just saw that you were walking the same path as me. I'm walking back home from a stroll in the forest." It wasn't a conventional greeting, but this girl is special. She has something that no one else can give Celest right now. Though no one will truly replace her mother, someone can make that void a little smaller is someone worth keeping around.

Celest's wave of heartfulness is cut short by the girl's brute response: "Listen kid, you shouldn't just tell strangers where you're headed. I don't know why you decided to approach me, but I don't have anything for you."

Ok. Celest was thrown off by her response. *This is what people must think about me.* "I'm not asking for anything. I just wanted to introduce myself. Anyway, I walk this path often so would you mind if I walked with you?"

The girl looks at Celest with confusion. "You *want* to walk with me?"

"Yes, I've seen you around. I know you live right next to me; I just didn't want to mention it in case it would scare you off."

The girl pauses. There is a long silence and then...*she's laughing?* The girl slowly chuckles. Her laugh almost sounds like a grumble. *She must be shy.*

The girl finally replies, "Yeah, it's a good thing you didn't lead with that. I walk over here every day. The woods are a wonderful place to think, you know? My name is Imani."

"I'm Celest," Celest says with a wide smile.

Celest and Imani continue to walk down the street. They talk about a few basic topics, age, beliefs, nothing extravagant. They come to a stop in front of both of their houses. *She's not so bad.*

"Well, we're home!" Celest bouncily announces.

Imani cooly responds, "We definitely are."

Imani turns around and starts to walk up her driveway and Celest does the same. *I hope we meet up again.* Celest opens her door and Buddy walks in. He grabs his stuffed bear. *You love that thing, don't you?* Celest goes directly to her room, climbs on her bed, and takes her notebook out once again. Buddy trots in the room beside her and tries to jump on the bed but he slips and falls back to the ground. *Goofball.* Celest sits up and taps her legs for Buddy to put his paws on. It's something he seemed to learn on his own over the years after comforting her so many times. He rests his paws in her lap and lets her place her book on the top of his head. Celest opens a new page:

I met a new person today. It was my neighbor right across the street from me. She said her name was Imani. She was pretty reserved and didn't seem to like me very much at first. She's older than me by two years. I hope I get to know her better.

Another long day. She changes into more comfortable clothes, lays down, and pulls the covers over her body. *Time to sleep.* Buddy goes over to his bed in the corner of the room. He grabs his stuffed bear, curls up and shuts his eyes. The sun falls.

***

Celest sits up, sliding the covers off her. Buddy greets her with a giant smile. *What should I do today?* She gets out of bed and whistles at Buddy to follow her. His head pops up and he rolls to his feet. Celest walks to the living room and glances to the left in the direction of her mom's room. *It's hard to go on without you.* She turns away and reaches for the door. Buddy runs in front of her and runs in place. *You're always excited to go on a walk.* Celest shows a smile. *Never change.*

They walk outside. Across the way, Imani is walking towards her house. *I never really asked about her dog.* Celest waves at her.

"Hey, how's it going?" Celest calls.

Imani smiles and walks over to Celest. Her dog wags its tail and goes right up to Buddy. Buddy tries to dart to the dog but is caught by his leash. Celest is knocked over by the force of Buddy's pull. She barrels straight through Imani. The dogs jump around and bark at each other while the two girls lay on the ground, scraped up from the fall. *Why do these things happen to me?* Celest struggles to stand up and holds out her hand for Imani who gladly takes it. They both brush themselves off. Celest looks to Imani to make sure she's ok. They both look behind them and see their dogs playing.

You're supposed to be on duty Buddy. What was that for? Celest looks at the tangle of gold and white closely. *So, she has a girl dog. A little bit bigger than buddy...an albino husky maybe. Big eyes, icy blue, and a huge smile.*

Imani notices Celest's interest in her dog, "This is Moonlight by the way. She's a bit of a goofball as you can see."

Moonlight. I like that name. Celest walks over to Moonlight and strokes her head. Moonlight licks her hand in response. *Why can't the world be more like these happy creatures?*

"So where are you headed?" Imani asks.

Celest looks up from the dogs and replies, "I'm just going out for a stroll."

"Just because?" Imani asks with a confused look.

Celest returns her look, "Yes?"

Imani looks to the side. Her shoulders began to hunch over, and her eyes return to the gaping stare Celest had first seen. The tone of her voice changes back to a low grumble. She mumbles out, "I wish my parents let me stroll around..."

But you're walking around right now? What is she talking about? Don't close off. We just met. Did I do something wrong? I don't know what I'm doing wrong. I tried just like she said. Breathe. Just breathe, it's fine.

"Hey it's ok. I know it's not the same, but you can always come with me if that makes you feel better," Celest's words flow out of her mouth without any real thought.

Imani reluctantly nods.

"C-can I come with you now?" she whispers out.

"Yes of course," Celest replies with the huge smile she's fabricated before. But this one *felt* real. *I feel like I'm really smiling. I'm not faking. I'm not-*

Buddy starts walking to the sound of Celest's whistle. *Did I tell him to start walking?* Imani walks beside her, holding Moonlight by her leash. *Why am I doing this? I am a good person though. So, should I be doing it because she needs help? She's afraid. But why? Is she like me? And why doesn't she want to go home? Is she in danger?*

Celest's mouth continues to move without instruction: "What's going on?"

Imani looks at Celest, confused. "What do you mean?" she says, no longer mumbling.

"Don't try to hide it from me," Celest argues, "Something is going on or you wouldn't have asked to walk with me."

Imani looks ashamed. "You wouldn't understand."

"You're right. I might not understand, but that doesn't mean I can't help you." *Where is this coming from?*

Imani pauses for a second and puts her hands in her pockets. *Something is definitely going on.* "You have a perfect family. I wish that my parents were gone every day."

Celest's tone sharpens, "What makes you think I have a perfect family?"

Imani, getting increasingly offended responds, "You can come and go as you please and you don't have any marks on you whatsoever!"

Marks? Celest takes a moment to examine herself. She is wearing a basic T-shirt and shorts, and her skin is perfectly clear. Anyone can see how she doesn't have any blemishes. Imani on the other hand is covered head to toe. Celest can't refute that Imani has these marks on her, but she knows she can't uncover her skin to find out.

Celest decides to let her frustrations out. "I'm sorry to tell you but I don't have a perfect family. My mother died, and my father was abusive. I don't even know where that guy is now."

Imani holds her tongue. She had no idea that Celest's life is as hard as hers. Celest does seem sad quite often, but she has such a huge personality that she assumed that she was ok. Imani is wrong.

"I-I'm so sorry," Imani croaks out.

"It's fine," Celest spits back. Celest looks to Buddy who smiles back at her. "As long as he's with me, I think I'll be ok."

They walk in silence the rest of their stroll. Eventually, Celest heads back in the direction of Aunt Marie's house. Nothing spectacular happens on the way there. When they do arrive, Buddy runs up to the door and barks. A few seconds later Aunt Marie answers the door.

"You're finished early tod-Oh!" Aunt Marie looks at Imani and her dog, "Who's this?"

Celest looks back to Aunt Marie with an unreadable expression and replies, "Auntie this is Imani, the girl you were talking about. She wanted to come over. Is that ok?"

Aunt Marie is taken aback at Celest's question. Not only did Celest bring someone over without asking, but she's also casually asking permission to let this girl stay in her house. To take it a step further, Celest hasn't spoken to anyone since her mom passed away. Why would she be willing to befriend someone so easily now? Despite her concerns, Aunt Marie is glad Celest took her advice. She needs someone in her life.

Aunt Marie maintains her stare. She steps back and holds the front door open with her body. Celest walks in, pausing for Imani who isn't following her. Celest grabs her hand and pulls her in the door. Imani bows when she passes Aunt Marie as a sign of respect or maybe as a sign of fear. Aunt Marie's stare can be unsettling.

Celest leads her new acquaintance to the living room couch. Imani is looking down the entire time, carefully taking each step. *Does she think the ground will crack or something? What is she thinking?* Celest attempts to hide her expression as she guides Imani to sit. She practically must push Imani over to get her to touch the couch at all. *What in the world?* She just shakes her head. *No need to make her feel worse about it.*

Aunt Marie still stands at the door. She takes a huge breath and closes her eyes for a moment. If Celest could see her, she wouldn't be able to tell what she was thinking, only that she was deep in thought. This only lasts a moment though, as she puts on her best smile and makes her way to the girls. After so many years in healthcare, this must be like clockwork to her.

Aunt Marie pulls one of the chairs from the dining room table and places it in front of the couch. She promptly sits on it, looking at Celest with confusion. Celest continues to awkwardly smile at Aunt Marie which only confuses her more. *Come on, you have to understand.* Buddy lays in his favorite spot in the living room, one of his many beds that Celest has placed for him. He looks to Moonlight who only lays on her owner's feet. *Like mother like daughter*. Buddy doesn't seem to pay them any mind, probably tired from playing with Moonlight earlier. He curls up contently.

There is a weird silence in the room. Aunt Marie cautiously voices, "Celest...May I speak with you for a moment?"

Celest nods. She turns to Imani and nods to her as well. *Ok just stay right there.* Imani doesn't look comfortable being in the house at all, but she's especially uneasy when she feels Celest rise off the couch and start walking down the hall. She folds her fingers together and sits perfectly still, eyes glued on Moonlight, the only familiarity in the room.

Celest and Aunt Marie make their way to what should have been Evelyn's room. It has been converted into a guest bedroom of sorts. Evelyn's things have been tidied up and the room is dusted and vacuumed regularly. Celest doesn't actually think Aunt Marie will invite guests to stay with her, but just in case, Aunt Marie makes sure the room looks nice. Celest gets lost in the feeling the room carries. Evelyn is long gone, but her aura stays.

"Would you like to explain to me why you have brought her to my house?" Aunt Marie asks.

"Well," Celest responds matter-of-factly, "You told me to talk to her. I talked to her right?"

Aunt Marie looks at Celest with piercing eyes. "Yes. I suppose I did," she finally says. She must have more to say but her lips tighten and nothing else comes out. *Well, that went better than I thought it would.*

Aunt Marie changes her tone again: "Ok. I'm going to let you go back in there, but don't *ever* bring someone in here unannounced like this. *Especially* if they have some animal with them. We don't know her. Don't do this again."

Celest nods. That's all she really can do. Aunt Marie doesn't throw Imani out, so it's a winning situation. She walks back towards the living room. As Celest rounds the corner of the hallway she notices the same shadowy figure sitting abnormally upright on the couch. *What is she doing?* Imani doesn't turn her head when they return. She just stares forward, but she knows they're there. *Uhh....okay..?*

Aunt Marie slides past Celest and asks Imani, "Have you eaten today?"

Imani turns her head to Aunt Marie but doesn't say anything still. She has the same expressionless face. *Stoic. Never changing.* "Uh..." she weakly speaks, "...I think I've eaten enough for today."

Celest and Aunt Marie share eyes for a moment. *She's lying.* Aunt Marie takes that as a cue to make her way to the kitchen and grab some pans. She paces for a few minutes thinking of what she can make for this girl. Celest always thought that habit of hers was cute. She always wants to prepare her best dishes for guests. She seems to settle on something after a while and begins filling one of her pots with water.

Aunt Marie asks Imani, "Any allergies honey?" She truly has the mind of a doctor.

Imani shakes her head no. She looks conflicted while she speaks, "Is it ok if I sleep?"

Is it ok if I sleep...? What kind of question is that?

Celest looks at Aunt Marie with a look of utter confusion. She continues to watch Aunt Marie nod to herself as if she was expecting Imani to ask her that question. She looks over her shoulder to make sure the food looked alright. Celest couldn't make out what it is, and it was too early for it to be smelling like anything. She then walks to the small closet in the hallway leading to Evelyn's room. She takes out a nice blanket and a matching pillow to give to Imani.

Imani looks like she doesn't quite know how to accept the courtesy. She carefully lays down, as if she was trying not to be seen. Her eyes never leave Aunt Marie's. She's watching, waiting, for something to happen. Nothing ever comes to pass. Celest gazes at Imani. *You get it.* That uncertainty isn't new to her; she knows it all too well.

Imani puts the pillow under her head and immediately falls asleep. *Strange girl...* Celest turns her attention back to Aunt Marie. She notices Aunt Marie's apron that reads, "Best Aunt in The World." *Mom must've given you that.* Celest faintly smiles at the thought of her mother, but it quickly fades. *Why didn't I notice?* She turns her head away from the kitchen. *I never change...* The tears fall down her face instantly. She can't help it, but it doesn't make her feel any better about crying. *Weak, just like her. Why do I still see you this way?* Memories wash over her in monstrous waves. *It was obvious. I should've seen it. I had no idea what you were going through. But I'm young. I'm not supposed to know, right? Why didn't you tell me? I want you here with me.* Celest feels a hand on her back, soothing her. She knows who it is, but can't bring herself to look at her.

"I forgive both of you for not telling me about her sickness. I understand why you did it," Celest randomly blurts out, "But I just wish I wasn't so blind."

Aunt Marie finds herself unable to speak. What is she going to say? They are both hurting after all this time. She tells herself that Celest is strong, but is she really? Celest is only a kid; she can only take so much. She continues to comfort Celest until she moves from the counter. Celest walks out of the room without saying a word. She goes into her room and cries. *Why am I here if you're not?*

***

"Celest? Celest. You've got to wake up now."

Celest forces her head from her bed. *What?* She squints her eyes open but can't make out anything around her. She is stuck in a haze. She rests her head once again only to be interrupted.

"No," Aunt Marie reminds her, "you have been asleep for a long time. You must wake up."

Celest groans. *I don't want to do anything at all. Why don't you just leave me alone?* Her body rises from the bed. *Why am I doing this anyway?* She haphazardly rolls her eyes around the room, not really searching for anything, but trying to regain control of herself.

She stares off saying, "Where is that girl? There was a girl here, right? Or..." She stops. *Was there a girl here? Or was that a dream? How long has it been?*

Aunt Marie calmly responds, "Yes, there was a girl here. After she woke up, she went home. She thanked both of us before she left and wanted you to know she is sorry for coming off as rude when you two met. Celest, that was a while ago. Are you sure you are not sick?"

A long time ago? That was like a couple hours ago. I went in my room, and I was crying. And then.... And then... I must've fallen asleep. Yeah, that must be what happened. I must've just fallen asleep. So, it has only been a couple hours at most. Celest notices the sunlight softly beaming into her room window. See? The sun is still out, so it hasn't been long.

"Aunt Marie, I'm not sure what you're talking about...I've only been asleep for-" Celest turns to address her caregiver, but she's not there. *What?*

She looks around the room, but no one is there. Her room is still and quiet. She checks the floor and finds Buddy sleeping in his little dog bed. *Why are you sleeping? Did she not wake you?* Celest touches her feet on the carpet and starts for her door, which is closed. *Didn't she come in the door? Why would she close it again?*

The door cracks open. She doesn't even realize that her hand turns the knob or that her arm pulls the door. It just opens. She steps out into the hall. She wants to call for Aunt Marie, but her voice is suddenly gone, as if something is weighing on her vocal cords. *Why is this happening? What do you want? What are you trying to tell me?* Celest is carried down the hall, toward her mother's old room. *No no no I don't want to go there!* Celest tries to stop herself, but it's as if something, some outside force, is pushing her forward. She can't stop it.

The force seems to respond to Celest though she doesn't speak to it. She takes a sudden turn into the art room. The first thing she notices is the darkness. It's unlike anything she has ever seen or has not seen. It feels familiar, but distant. There is a strange glow in the middle of the room. It's not bright, but Celest can't seem to make out what's in it. She takes a step in the light's direction. Every step she takes, the harder it becomes. She feels like she is walking through an ocean; she's getting closer, but everything around her is holding her back. The light is beckoning to her still.

Celest's mind is racing. She is thinking everything and nothing at once. *What do you want to tell me? What am I missing?* She finally makes her final strides to the light. She reaches forward to try and touch this mysterious illumination only for it to fade out when she makes contact with it. She tilts her head to one side, trying to figure out what she is seeing. In place of the light is Evelyn's painting. The painting itself adopts the glow it had so long ago. Celest examines the painting but can't focus on it entirely. The glow isn't strong enough. She tries her hardest to make out every detail of it.

The house, the stars, the moon, the night sky. And the girl... Celest squints her eyes even harder than before. *The house, the stars, the moon, the night sky, and...the girl... Where is the girl?* Celest feels her body tense. Chills begin to run down every bone in her body. *Something is wrong. The girl, why is she not there? And why are you showing me this now? What is happening?* Her vision begins to fade. She struggles against it in vain. She is fighting death itself. The walls around her close in and feel like they are constricting every ounce of breath she has left. *No! I need more time! Just a little more time! I don't understand! Give me time to understand! Don't do this again!*

"Celest let's go! You're going to be late!"

What?

Celest sits up again. She is back in her room. *What is going on?* The light shines through her window once again. Buddy is trotting around the room, excited to leave the house. *The door...* The door is wide open. Celest bolts out of her room. *Where is the girl?* She barrels through the art room's doorway and flips the lights on. The painting is there in its original spot. It looks completely normal. *The house, the stars, the moon, and the girl. They're all here.*

"Celest what are you doing!? Aunt Marie yells.

Celest ignores Aunt Marie's concern. *What time is it?* "What time is it?" she asks as Aunt Marie walks behind her.

Aunt Marie responds in a harsh tone, "Why are you acting like this Celest? We've been over this. You have to get up earlier to get ready for school."

School...? "What do you mean school?" she asks.

Aunt Marie annoyedly looks at her. She responds, "You know good and well that you have to get up every Monday morning to go to school. Don't play like this with me. You've gotten up every Monday morning for the past however many years and went to school. That's not changing today."

Celest is unresponsive to Aunt Marie's tone. *Something is wrong.* "Where is Imani?" she asks for the second time.

Aunt Marie briskly walks to the living room to collect Celest's backpack and binders. She probably packed lunch for her already as well. "You haven't invited her over in quite a while. That's a good question. It's been a little bit since you have seen her..." she says in between lifting things.

I saw her yesterday. Or last week? Or sometime recently. I just met her. What is she talking about?

"Now let's go," Aunt Marie says firmly, "You won't be late to school again."

Celest mindlessly nods and grabs her stuff from Aunt Marie. She can't understand what has happened recently, but she can't be confused forever. She will figure it out eventually. Her legs carry her to the front door. She glances down at Buddy. *Always happy...always smiling...If only I was that way...* She grabs his leash, and they are out the door as if nothing happened. *Everything is fine. It'll stop soon. It'll stop. It has to.*

Chapter 9: All the Same, Nothing Different

Celest's feet carry her over the landscape. They float her mindlessly in the right direction. *Taller, taller, shorter, taller, removed...* Celest recounts the trees which have grown and shrunk with time. She has been doing this often lately. It helps her take her mind off things...or keep her mind on things. She never really decided to start doing it, it just happened, and she doesn't question it. Though, she doesn't question much these days. *This would be a great time to write*, she thinks, but if she actually pulls out her notebook...she does not know.

I walk on this path alone again. It feels quite strange, yet the same. I don't feel sad today, I just feel nothing. I don't really remember the last thing I felt per se... Our neighbors seem to be caring for their respective foliage except for one of them, but they have never been able to keep their house lively. It's just who they are. Just like I am. I could never keep anyone around me lively.... Maybe if you were here, you'd tell me different. Maybe you could spring me back to life, but until then...today is just another day...in a series of days...in a series of years... Nothing is different and everything is the same.

Celest's school is about a mile from her house or at least she thinks it is. She can't remember the last time she asked Aunt Marie how far away her school is. *I must've mentioned it when I first started walking there...* It doesn't matter. She allows herself to be carried through the neighborhood. Buddy bounces around next to her, enjoying nature. *What I'd give to be like you...* However far away her school is from her house, it doesn't take long for Celest to be staring at its front entrance.

The black gates never quite seemed to welcome Celest. They seem quite daunting with their pointed ends and large locks. The beige concrete walls are nice, never blemished, never cracked. The path beneath her feet ages with time. Old gum and dirt decorate it so bountifully. Hundreds of thousands of children have come before Celest and thousands more will follow her. *So, what is so significant about me?* Children are scattered about, chatting to their friends. Others are reading, drawing, or napping on the benches scattered about. *Just one more kid running through this school...Just like the others...All the same...*

Celest arrives at room 302, the art room. Today is part of her curriculum fair. Her school holds this event once per year to get students interested in different extracurriculars. The arts teacher always offers a weeklong class for incoming students and veteran students who want to pursue the arts. *One more year...* Celest lets herself in and beelines to a table. She sets her bags down just as quickly and commands Buddy to sit on the floor next to her. She pulls out a sheet of paper from her bag that she has already written on. *Red, violet, brown, pink.* She looks up from the paper after studying it a while and searches the room for paints.

She once again commands Buddy, this time to stay still as she walks to the supply cart on the other side of the room. She shuffles out of her seat only to bump into something rushing past. *Watch where you're going.* Celest doesn't even try to investigate what she's run into. She tucks her head and continues her mission to retrieve her paints. *Don't say anything. Don't say anything. Just leave me alone.*

Celest shudders at a screeching "Excuse you!" She turns to see what or *who* she had accidentally run into and to her annoyance it is a girl she has known for far too long. This girl always strutted around the school wanting all the attention from the little boys who would always follow her around. She is such a stuck-up little girl that the mention of her name infuriates Celest. It doesn't help that she has one of those names associated with those like her either. Celest can't stand to look at Av-

"What do you want?" Celest replies abruptly and angrily.

Av...A...Hm...What is her na- It doesn't matter! Leave me alone! Celest is fighting with her own thoughts. It almost feels as if her soul is being split in two. She knows who she is or who she is *supposed* to be, but there is another part of her that just wants to be seen, who just wants to be let out. Who cares what this girl thinks or how she will impact her, Celest is just angry. She's angry at the world for taking so much from her, yet never seeming to be satisfied. Taking the only family she had left. Ripping her mom away from her-

"Move," Celest hisses at this girl.

Of course, the girl uses this opportunity to try and poke fun at Celest, but it is nothing new. Celest throws a few insults, and the girl was off finding a new target to torment. Although she is an outcast, Celest has never been the type of person to allow someone to talk down to her. She is far too used to that. *These people never change...so shallow*. After her quick interaction, Celest fetches her paints as intended and sits back at her table ready to continue her masterpiece.

She is largely uninterrupted during this time. She gets lost in her work, pouring every emotion into her art, something Aunt Marie taught her how to do. Every brush stroke is like a release of energy that has been pent up for so long. She never wants to stop painting. The canvas is the only one who knows her true feelings. Why would she ever want to give that up?

And so, she continues painting and painting, occasionally reaching down to pet her companion. She takes a snack break after finishing the background of her current painting. She cleans her brushes a few times, transitioning into the foreground of the piece. Besides these small interruptions, her mind is singular, and she can think to herself. But, after a long moment of silence, she finally looks up.

A small crowd has formed in one of the corners of the room. *A new member.* The art teacher always forces the returning participants to introduce themselves, which doesn't really make sense to Celest. *Why not allow them to be genuine?* But authenticity doesn't earn the grade. Celest rolls her eyes. *Here we go again. I'd probably scare them off...* She drags her feet in the crowd's direction. Might as well get it over with.

She gets behind a girl near the outside of the circle as to not intrude on the newcomer's space, though they didn't have much of it now. The crowd seems to almost swallow the being inside it with hands flying out in gestures and random words mixing into a chaotic vocalization. Celest can barely make out the person garnering all this attention but does manage to get a glimpse through the crowd. It is a girl with long, flowing, bright orange hair. *She seems small.*

Celest stops trying to look in the middle of the crowd and looks at the crowd itself. *Why now? Why so many people? What is goi-* She can't even finish asking herself what was happening in front of her before a memory snaps into her mind. Instead of this girl, she sees herself. She sees a small, insecure little Celest being bombarded with questions about her family and the girl not being able to answer. *What do you do for fun? Do you go on family trips? What is your favorite meal your parents cook you? What do you do with your family on the weekends? You know, you never really talk about your mom.*

"Why won't you speak?"

"Yeah, what's your problem? Can't you hear us?"

"You can't ignore us forever."

And just like that, she snaps.

Celest doesn't have time to think of what she's going to say or why she's having this protective feeling for this girl. She doesn't exactly remember how she got to the center of the circle with this girl, but she announces something with a furry she hasn't felt in years. It's not a particularly threatening phrase but Celest's voice rings throughout the room.

"Leave her alone!"

Silence finally. The room drops. It's like Celest just announced that the moon was falling to earth. Everyone stares at her in shock. Most of them had not heard her mutter a word since being in the art club. Celest looks around her and begins to see pointed eyebrows and glares. *Of course. There's always a problem.* The sly comments and jeers redirect to Celest. *Why is no one else seeing this?* She looks out to meet her teacher's eyes, but she isn't at her desk. *What a time to be in your office...* She quickly gives up on that option and drowns the comments out. After everything that has happened to her, a group of kids attempting to ridicule her is not going to be the thing to take her out.

Celest simply grabs the girl's hand and broods her way through the crowd. She doesn't really think anything. She is only worried about getting to her destination. Everything seems to move in slow motion, like some kind of movie montage or an important scene in a book. She can hear all the insults and see all of the hands waving, but they seem so far away. Was this really happening? She squeezes the girl's hand subconsciously. *It's real.* Celest doesn't know why she wants to save this girl so badly. That voice that has been haunting her recently, the one that eerily feels like her mother, feels like it is pushing her to do these things. She is not leading this girl away from the crowd, her body is carrying both of them away. It's not a logical decision. She doesn't think about it.

And yet, even though she doesn't understand it, they end up back at the secluded table where Celest first sat down. She still doesn't speak. *What would I even say?* The new girl looks under the table to see Buddy laying on his front two paws. She has this confused but unreadable expression on her face. *Doesn't like animals maybe?* Celest doesn't dwell on the girl's awkward stature. She seems like she has had enough to deal with.

Celest simply sits down and continues her painting where she left off. To be honest, the painting is already done, but she just wants to make the girl feel safe. *I get it.* The girl isn't particularly responsive to this. She just stares at Celest which was a bit unsettling. *How am I supposed to focus when you're looking at me like that?* She quickly gives up on her original idea.

Celest puts her canvas down and instead takes out her journal. She turns to a blank page and begins to sketch. *Just a past time really. I'm not good at drawing yet. It'll take my mind off her staring.* Celest gets lost in her imagination and sketches a waterfall flowing over some rocks. It's a simple sketch, nothing fancy, but she's proud of herself.

While focused on her own creativity, Celest must have missed the new girl setting her things down and pulling out her own sketchbook. The girl quickly drags her pencil across her paper almost as if she is dancing with it; it's a tango only she could understand. It really is an amazing sight. She knows exactly what she wants and knows how to transfer it to her pages. Celest would be staring in awe if she wasn't so engrossed in her drawing.

The rings of the girl's sketchbook scrape across the table as it slides in front of Celest. She finally looks up. *Huh?* The girl is looking back at her with a little upturn in the corners of her mouth. It's not that noticeable, as if she is afraid to smile, but Celest notices it. She has a knack for noticing things like that. *Whoa.* Celest looks to the book to only be staring at herself. The girl had created a perfect sketch of her and Buddy smiling at each other. *How did you-?* The girl seems amused at Celest's face. She lets out a funny laugh before returning to her stoic expression.

"This is great," Celest says.

The girl nods. Although Celest would like to know her better, she doesn't force her to speak. *Maybe it's just not her thing.* Celest continues to have this indifferent attitude towards the girl. She simply doesn't care if she speaks to her or not. She just wants the girl to be happy. *I don't know why...* she thinks, *but I just want her to be happy.*

It's not like I know her or anything about her, I just want her to be alright. I don't know why. It doesn't make sense, but it's true. I just want her to be ok. Maybe it was the stoic look on her face. Maybe it was how the others were ganged up on her. Maybe it was because she was so small. Maybe it was how she was alone. Maybe it was how there was no one to save her. Maybe it was how she was drowning. Maybe it was how the others didn't care.

Perhaps it's just who I am...or perhaps it is because I never was.

Celest thinks about the girl intently as if she is trying to solve the world's hardest jigsaw puzzle. She doesn't speak of course, as she usually doesn't. Now is not the time to break convention.

Her hands settle on the table. She returns her gaze to the girl to find her smiling in her direction. *Why are you...?* Before Celest can finish her thought, she looks to where the girl is gazing: her journal. Celest stares at it in awe. A detailed sketch of the girl appeared on the page. *I didn't...* The girl lets out a laugh. It's broken and strange, but it's genuine. She has the most beautiful smile. Celest grins at the way the girl's freckles seem to bounce on her cheeks.

The girl reaches over and slides Celest's journal close to her so she can look at the drawing herself. She continues to grin while looking over it. *She looks so happy. Nothing like she did before. Well, that's...different...* The girl takes her pencil and writes something at the bottom of the page and then slides it back across the table. Celest reads over what she wrote. The girl signed "Pep" with a heart.

Pep. Celest feels like this is an important moment, but she doesn't know why. *Pep. Like Pepper. I'll remember your name.* But of course, this moment doesn't last long. *Nothing nice does.* One of the girls that was picking on Pep taps Celest on the shoulder. She is shorter than Celest by a couple inches. She has long, brown hair that she always flaunts at everyone. She has freckles as well, but they're not as light as Pep's. Celest might've actually found them pretty if her personality wasn't so crude. *First you insult me, then this girl, now you're back to me again. Make up your mind.*

Celest never understood why people had time for things like that, but maybe that's because she always had important things to worry about like how she was going to protect her mom. Petty things like this don't interest Celest. Usually she ignores them, but today she is done. The overwhelming feeling of no feeling overtook her this day and she lost any desire to walk away. *You want to play games? I can play too.*

Celest looks under the table and signals Buddy to stay. *I need to be alone.* She then quickly stands, lightly brushing the girl's shoulder. One of the girl's friends is close behind her, glaring. *Smaller, weaker, slower....*

"So," the first girl says, "You think you're better than us?"

A corner, the hallway, the supply rooms...

"You gonna answer me brat?"

Too visible, won't hurt, too much damage...

"We're talking to you idiot!"

Long hair...supply closet...not noticeable...

Celest finally meets eyes with both of the girls. She chuckles to herself and walks away. Buddy's head swivels and he watches his owner leave the table. The girls are surprisingly quiet during Celest's little stroll. She walks into a supply closet where all the extra art supplies are kept. Pottery, portraits, sculptures, and other artworks are spread throughout the room. *You're going to close the door behind us.*

Just as Celest thought, the girls close the closet door behind them. They start talking some nonsense about how Celest was insulting them by talking to Pep. *If it really mattered to you, all you had to do was be nice to her. You're wasting your time.* They continue to throw random insults her way, but she doesn't feel them. She stares blankly at them. *Always the same thing... I'm doing something wrong by existing. That's all they ever say. Broken records.*

"Are you done?" Celest blankly asks.

The girls look surprised. "Excuse me?" one says.

"Are you done talking now? I'm sick of it. Yeah, I think I'm better than you. You're all garbage. Now can I leave? I answered your little question," Celest clarifies.

The girls waste no time getting in Celest's face. Celest doesn't recall what they say after this. She just remembers what she was thinking.

Long hair...supply closet...no one will notice.

And then she snaps. She grabs a fist full of hair from the girl closest to her and just starts yanking. *You're going to leave me alone.* Celest pulls and tugs and tears this girl's hair out. Chunks are falling to the floor, and she doesn't fight it or at least she is not strong enough to get out of Celest's grip. Her friend just stands still. She doesn't even try to help her. *Strange. It's almost as if fear doesn't make good friends.*

Celest keeps going until she feels that the girl has had enough. She couldn't pull out too much; she didn't need there to be evidence. Just enough to teach her a lesson. When she finally lets go, the girl whimpers and rushes out a side door connected to the closet. *She doesn't want to be embarrassed in front of everyone.* Her "friend" follows close behind. *Predictable.*

Celest looks around and finds some supplies to pick up and walks back into the main room. No one seems to notice her disappearance. She calmly walks back to her and Pep's table. Pep is petting Buddy as he rests his head in her lap. *You know you're not really supposed to play with a medical dog like that...* Ignoring her instincts to tell Pep to leave Buddy alone and to stop distracting him from his duty, Celest simply sits back at her seat. She looks down and takes a heavy breath. *Can't you just leave me alone? ....No of course not...*

Celest turns her gaze to her own body. Her arms, legs, and torso are unscathed minus a red mark on her right wrist from the girl gripping her so hard. *What did you gain from that?* She looks around the room one more time, just to make sure, but again no one pays her any attention. The cluster of bullies had disbursed while she was gone and are now back to doing art. Some were painting, others were writing, and others were sculpting, as if nothing had happened a few minutes before. *Lost interest huh?*

Celest packs her area up. *It's early, but Aunt Marie will understand.* She takes all the supplies she used as a cover back into the supply closet. She sees a couple clumps of the girl's hair where they stood before. She contemplates disposing of it, but eventually decides against it. That might seem suspicious. She swiftly walks back to the table and shoves the rest of her things into her bag. Pep watches her with a confused look. Celest whistles. Buddy turns his head and trots to Celest's side. Finally, she hoists her bag up on her shoulders, turning to leave.

"Where are you going?" Pep interjects. Her voice is very faint and fragile.

Celest contrasts with her strong expression, "I'm leaving."

Pep doesn't speak for a moment. Her face returns to the unreadable expression Celest saw in her before. *What is it?* She looks down at the table, at what Celest assumes is a new drawing she completed while she was dealing with the two girls. Silently, Pep grabs the paper and extends her arm out to Celest. *Do you want me to have it?* Celest stares, a bit confused at the figure in front of her. *She's not looking at me so...*

Pep looks up from the table. She nudges the paper closer to Celest who takes it this time. *Thanks...* Celest flips the page over to find that it is Pep's drawing of her. Pep's signature is in the bottom right of the paper, smaller than it was on Celest's drawing. *This is different...* Pep flashes a smile while Celest makes her way to the exit. *I don't think I've had anyone do this for me before. That's not normal. It's probably a trick. Just like everyone else. But her eyes were different. Her nature was different. She was differe- No. No, she wasn't. She's just the same as everyone else. They all leave in the end. I shouldn't get my hopes up. Or maybe...*

***

"So how was it," Aunt Marie asks enthusiastically.

Celest throws her bag on the living room floor. She doesn't look at her aunt. *Why do you even ask me that? You know I will always have the same answer. Nothing. Ever. Changes.* She ignores Aunt Marie entirely, dragging her feet to the couch and plopping herself down. At least, that is likely what happened. Celest just remembers being on the couch hearing Aunt Marie ask the same annoying questions she does every day. *So how was school? How was your day?* It's always the same. In the same fashion, Celest's responses never change.

Celest's hand flips through the TV stations. She's not really looking for anything to watch, but it is routine at this point. She might not even recognize that she is scrolling. "Wasn't great," she responds flatly, still switching through stations. She rests her left hand on Buddy's head. *When did you get on the couch?*

Aunt Marie's smile fades for a moment but she makes sure to return to her original expression. After all the days Celest has come home like this, it doesn't really make sense that she still continues to smile at her. Celest is waiting for the day when Aunt Marie lashes out at her or leaves her. *Everyone else has done it.*

Celest thinks about the last thought she had. *Well, I guess everyone hasn't. Imani still speaks to me whenever I see her walking Moonlight and the girl from today doesn't really seem to have a reason to leave. I mean why would either of them leave me? Do they even have anything else to go back to? That's kinda harsh, but I know I'm right. I am the same way. I never asked to be left. I never wanted people to leave. Well....maybe dad, but that's a different case. I would never leave anyone because I don't have anyone. So why do they always leave me? Do they have better people to be with? It's possible. I'm not really the greatest person. But mom didn't have anything, and she still left me. She didn't want to, but she did. They all leave in the end. It's nothing different. It's all the same. No matter what happens, they always leave. So, when will you leave me Aunt Marie?*

Celest's mouth begins to move. Her voice comes out raspy and flat, much like her visage. "Do you remember how you used to tell me that some kids just hate others for no reason?" she asks.

The question is a bit ironic. Aunt Marie can argue that Celest has hated her for no reason.

"Yes, I remember." Aunt Marie responds in no particular tone. "Why do you ask?"

"Well," Celest starts, "I believe you now."

Aunt Marie waits for Celest to say more, but nothing follows her previous statement. She is patient though, and responds with compassion. *As usual...* She knew about the girls bothering Celest. She expected something like that to happen at Celest's age. The school she goes to is predominantly white and it is known that the kids don't particularly like their black classmates. Of course, she was right in thinking this way. The only people who ever messed with Celest were the pretentious white girls who thought they were better than everyone else there.

Aunt Marie speaks, "Unfortunately, we don't get the same luxuries as other people. I know you didn't do anything to them, but that's how life is for us. You should stay proud of who you are." She stops for a second before she starts to smile. "So," she playfully asks, "Did you get her?"

Even in her perpetual mood, Celest can't help but smile at Aunt Marie's words. She is a sweet old lady, but Celest can tell she used to be a lively young girl. *Oh, I got her alright. Won't be bothering me anymore.* Celest doesn't answer Aunt Marie, but her expression says all she needs to know. Aunt Marie nods in satisfaction.

"You know, I met a girl today." Celest randomly mentions. *I might as well tell her about it. Why not? Maybe she'll be different.*

"Oh, you met a girl?" Aunt Marie says with a tinge of coyness in her voice.

Celest stops flipping through the channels. She places her hand on Buddy's head which was now in her lap. It's a nervous habit she picked up. *Yes, I met a girl...Not like that.* "She was new to the art fair this year. Did I tell you there was an art fair? Anyways, I was doing what I usually do and just moped around a little bit. That one girl came over to me and started bothering me, but I just brushed her off right? Yeah, so then I was finishing up some paintings I had but something was a little off. Those girls hadn't come up to bother me in a while and I looked up and saw that there was a circle forming around one section of the room. I looked over to see if our teacher was paying attention to it, but she was completely gone! She just wasn't there at all! So of course I was confused, but I didn't really want to be a part of that, so I got back doing what I was doing. Eventually, I did actually go over there and look because I was being nosey and guess what I saw?! There was this small girl in the middle of this circle and they were all hurling insults at her! She wasn't even doing anything! She was just standing there. She seemed so small. Granted she *is* really small. I mean you should really see her, she's tiny. Anyways, I got super upset at them because this girl was clearly new and she wasn't even saying anything. Then I went in there and pulled her out. I sat her at my table and she turned out to be a good person. She's weird, but she's nice and sweet. After that happened two of the girls I was talking about before came over and wanted to bother me again so I took them into one of the closets and ripped one of the girls' hair out. They left after that-"

Aunt Marie's face is utterly confused. She looks like someone just asked her to solve the mystery of life. *Oh...Must've been rambling...* Aunt Marie is completely frozen.

"So," Aunt Marie says stiffly, "you went to this art fair....and you helped a girl who was being....teased....and then you went and ripped a girl's hair out....whose been bothering you....for a while...?"

Celest nods. Aunt Marie responds in the same astonished tone, "Ok..." She wants to say more, but she doesn't know where to start. Celest never speaks to anyone, let alone give an entire recount of her day.

Celest becomes embarrassed. *Shouldn't have said anything...* Letting her emotions out scares her in a way she can't really describe. How would she? She's never had the opportunity to really express herself without being labeled or ignored. Expressing emotions is something that must be learned and Celest is years behind.

They both stand there, staring at each other. It is a strange sight, but neither of them know how to deal with this situation.

Celest is the first to break the eye contact. "I'll...just go..." she squeaks out. Before Aunt Marie can protest, Celest darts to her room and locks her door behind her. *What was that? What was I thinking?* She can feel her heartbeat in her ears. She leans up against her door. *She's going to leave. She's going to leave. She's going to leave. She's going to leave. She's going to leave. She's-*

"Um...Are you ok in there?"

She's going to leave.

"Celest it's ok if you don't want to talk about it."

She's going to leave.

"We can always talk about something else."

She's going to leave.

"We can talk about my day instead? I had a really nice medical student come shadow me today."

She's going to leave.

"Stop! Leave me alone! I don't care about your day! I don't care what you have to say!" Celest roars.

There isn't another response for a while. Celest waits and waits, but Aunt Marie isn't there. Celest is sitting with her back to her door. *Surely, she'll come back. She always does. It's annoying, but she always comes back. That can't just be it.* Celest waits some more. She waits so long that the sky changes color. It's not nighttime, but it will be soon. *She will answer. She will answer.* Celest looks to Buddy for comfort only to see that he is sleeping in his dog bed. *Has it been that long?*

That's the thing that Celest never understands. Everything has always ended the same for her. *Anyone I ever trust ends up leaving.* It doesn't matter how. It doesn't matter when. They always leave. Anyone she ever trusts ends up leaving. She had to have trusted her father at one point. Babies don't come with hatred. *Anyone I ever trust ends up leaving.* That man that Celest trusted as a baby has been gone for so long that she can't even remember who he was. And now, he's literally been gone for years. No birthdays. No holidays. No anything. Never a "How are you doing?" or an "I miss you." Nothing. *Anyone I ever trust ends up leaving. He doesn't even care. He got away. He's probably living a grand life with a whole other family.* Her grandparents left her when they abandoned her mom. Never got a chance to meet them. *It wasn't my fault!* But, as always, anyone she ever trusts ends up leaving. Her mom was really all she had. She tried to protect Celest the best she could, but it was impossible. She was too deep in her own situation. Celest never saw her mother for who she was because of all the pain. She hated her mom for being so weak. But they were stuck together. Just her and her mom. And then it was just her. *Anyone I ever trust ends up leaving. She got to escape, but she left me here.* And even now, she knows that she never really hated her mom. She hated the pain around her. She hated the abuse. She just had to get it out somehow. Her mom was an easy target. *Anyone I ever trust ends up leaving.* But now there is no one. Aunt Marie wanted to be there for her, but Celest never let her. She has given all she has to Celest but that wasn't good enough for her. She was too afraid that it was a hoax. And now she's gone. *Anyone I ever trust ends up leaving. I can't keep anyone. I'm not good enough for anyone. I'm so horrible that they all leave. No one will stay for me. Anyone I ever trust ends up leaving.*

Tears. Rain. Pour. Waterfall. Typhoon. "Why doesn't anyone stay!?" she yells. It doesn't matter. No one is there to hear it anyway. Why not scream? "Why does nobody love me?! Am I just a temporary phase that people get tired of after so long? Am I so bad that they can't stand it?! What is wrong with me?!"

She tries to yell out more. She tries to tell the world how she feels, but she can't. Her sobs are so deep that nothing comes out. She just sobs to herself, to God, to anyone who is listening. *Are you listening? Or have you left me too?* Celest sits with her thoughts. *I don't have anyone left. No one can hear me. No one tries to listen. No one is here. I am alone. I don't deserve anyone, and I'll never be anyone. I'll always be the same. Life will always be the same. Wake up. Go to school. Come back. Cry. Wake up. Go to school. Come back. Cry. Wake up. Go to work. Come back. Cry. Some more crying here, some moping there. There is no point. There is no point in my life. There never will be. No one can change that.*

For a brief moment, a split second, Celest's mind goes blank. There is nothing else to say. There is no point. There is no happy ending. There is no lesson. It is just an endless cycle. That moment allows her to feel reality. For just that moment, she thinks she can hear something shuffling around on the other side of her door. It is subtle, like it is trying to sneak away from her, but it is clear. There is a shuffle and then steps getting farther and farther away from her room.

Something was listening.

Chapter 10: Reality

The sun shines through the window just like any other day. Despite all that happened last night, the sun still shines without fail. *Always the same. Never changing...*

Celest sits up. She slowly cranes her head around the room. *A tennis ball, my clothes, a book.* But Celest isn't really looking for anything. Or maybe she is. It doesn't matter. *Nothing does.* She eventually rests her eyes on Buddy who is standing next to her bed. He also looks back to her, noticing that she had awakened. Normally, Celest would point out how strange it was that Buddy had woken up before her, but today is different. She can't put her finger on why, but today is one of a kind.

Celest makes no comment on Buddy's strange behavior. In fact, she makes no comments at all. Even her mind has gone silent besides it occasionally identifying things in the room. *My backpack, the dog bed, my sheets.* It's very surreal. Celest can't even tell if she is awake or not.

She gets out of her bed nonetheless. Why not? Immediately she knows that she is not in control. The world is hazy, and she can't think. Her body is moving itself again. This would probably be a time where she would think *why does this keep happening to me?* But again, no thoughts are forming. It's like someone has tied a gag around her brain. She goes along with her puppeteer in acquiescence.

Her legs swing over her bedside. Her hips rise off the bed. Her body stands. Buddy joins by her side as he was trained to do. Celest can almost relate to him in a way. He doesn't think, he just does. He doesn't know why he's supposed to be around Celest all the time, he just is. That's what his body was trained to do. Her body is trained for this moment.

Buddy trots out the door and out of sight. Celest's eyes move with him, and her legs follow. She can feel how heavy the house is. Once again, she feels as if she is moving underwater. Nothing is in focus. The first thought she has is *Will I see the lights again?* She is referring to that mysterious glow that she has encountered a couple times. She still doesn't know what it is, but she knows it's the only thing that is telling her to keep going.

Celest is brought to the dining room table. She turns her eyes to the ground to see what has stopped Buddy, only for him not to be there. Her mind doesn't allow her to question why Buddy has randomly disappeared. He's not in the living room or the kitchen or in the hall. He couldn't have traveled any farther than that, yet he isn't here. Celest's shoulders orient back to the dining room table. She can see a little note left behind. Her body gives her just enough control to drag her eyes across the page.

You should take the day off. I'm going off to work and I will be back at the end of the day. Just relax.

-Marie

Celest doesn't dwell on the note for long. She should be at school, and she debates going, but ultimately, she listens to Aunt Marie. There's no way to know why Aunt Marie decided to let Celest skip school today. It could be a sign, or a coincidence, or maybe something else. It doesn't matter. Celest is here now.

And she's alone.

I shouldn't be alone.

Celest knew this would happen eventually. She would get caught by herself and no one would be there to catch her. There is no one here to stop her. No one will save her.

Celest starts to sweat. *There's no one to save me.* Her head turns to the front door. One after the other, Celest's feet force her closer and closer to the door. To her surprise, it stops there. The door is staring at her. *It's my choice. I have to open it.* But Celest doesn't open it. She can only stare at it. There's more to be done. She turns away and looks to the art room.

Celest chooses to go to the art room. She is in control. *It has to be there.* She pushes and claws through the weight surrounding her. One step at a time, she makes her way to the doorway. She feels for the light switch, but her hand falls away before she flips it on. *It'll be here.* She ignores the darkness as she speeds towards the center of the room. *It'll be here.*

Celest stares into nothing. There is nothing there, but she hoped. She hoped she would see a sign that would tell her she was crazy. She wanted, no she *needed,* to see that mysterious glow again. Just one more time. *If it was real, it would show itself. It will tell me not to do it.*

Nothing happens.

Celest is left alone in the pitch-black room. There are no lights, no windows, no one, and nothing to speak to her. This is it. There is nothing. There is no point. There is no reason for her to be here anymore. Nothing to look forward to. Everything is the same as everything else. Everything is darkness. There is no light. There is nothing.

And so she waits.

And waits

And waits

And waits

And waits

And waits

But nothing ever happens. No one ever comes to save her. She is alone. She is alone for good.

***

It'll be fine if I was gone. It'll be fine if I were to just fade away. Buddy would be fine. He probably wouldn't even miss me. He's just a dog, right? He wouldn't even remember me. Aunt Marie... She's a doctor. She is trained for these things. Besides, I'm just another patient to her. I mean that is what I am right? I was just a sickly little child that happened to come into her care. She just so happened to take me in, but she would've done that for anyone else.

Celest tussles with her thoughts. Aunt Marie will be ok. She has to be, logically. She has been a doctor for many years and has lost several patients. She'll just be another statistic. She gets on the floor and peers under her bed. It's dark, but she can see what she expected to find under there: a little note filled with her handwriting. She grabs the note and swings her legs out from under herself so she can read it comfortably.

I don't even feel like I wrote these words anymore. I can't remember the last time I looked at them, but I know they are always there. I've thought about using you before, but I've always been too afraid. But what is there to fear now? No one is here for me. I have nothing to lose. I guess I could say I have myself to lose, but where has she gone? I don't even think there is a me. There is just this shell that I call myself.

It doesn't take Celest long to figure out that today is the day. She received a message from God that this is what is meant to happen. Aunt Marie is out of the house, no one answered her cries last night, and whatever connection she has to that strange phenomena He likes to send her way is nonexistent. This is the time and there will never be another time more perfect than this.

Celest gets up and casually walks to the kitchen table. She sets her note down next to Aunt Marie's, a sort of offering to her. *She'll see it as soon as she gets back.* She then makes her way to the art room once again, this time turning on the lights. *Still have nothing to say? Not going to stop me?* Celest does have a great sense of disappointment in her gut. *How could you just let me go?* But that doesn't deter her from her mission. She continues on as if she is going out on a morning stroll. There is no alarm. There is no concern. There is no fear. There is nothing. There are no emotions and there is no Celest. There is just a walking shell pretending to be a little girl with hopes. A shell pretending that it could be anything more than something made to shield others. A shell that can mimic, but can never create.

She lifts the tall ladder that Aunt Marie uses to use to reach the paintings high on the walls and rests it on the side of her body. Using this leverage, she walks through the house and out the front door. She rounds a corner of the house and heads straight to the back yard. The gate is open for her, inviting her through. *Bet you wish you would've closed that....* Through the gate Celest goes. She props the ladder up on the back of the house. Again, she does this with no emotions, no care to get tired, no care to stop because of the pain. She does briefly look around her feet to see if Buddy has come to talk some sense into her, but he's still missing. *Alright,* she thinks, *this is it.*

The climb to the roof is not pleasant exactly. Celest still feels largely indifferent about what she's about to do, but she can't help but notice how red her hands are from carrying the ladder and how much her side hurts from one of the edges digging into her skin. It's not a present pain, it's as if she is watching someone else getting hurt and she is just wincing out of anticipation. But it's ok. None of it actually matters. *It'll be over soon.* Despite telling herself that her pain is irrelevant, Celest's hands still shake as she grips the ladder. Her legs tremble as she gets higher and higher off the ground. *When will I reach the top?*

Of course, she reaches the end of the ladder. *Everything has an end.* She uses her arms to reach the ledge of the house and pull herself up. The roof tiles scrape against Celest's smooth skin. Well, they are as smooth as they can be...she hasn't particularly cared to wear lotion every day. She covers her arms when she goes out anyway. What's the point?

Once she pulls herself on top of the roof, she stares off into the sky. *Surely someone will see me and order me down.* She once again counts the trees and flowers. Aunt Marie's flowers are due to be watered. They look a little dried out and slightly discolored. *Just like me.* She sits and scoots herself to the edge of the roof, facing the backyard. She is not so visible where anyone could find her, but she isn't completely hidden. She doesn't want to be stopped. Not exactly anyways...

I have always known that my life was weird. I never really had anything to live for. I guess they won't really be able to say much about me at the funeral. If there even is a funeral... No one is left to even give me one. I'll probably just be scooped up by some policeman and sent to a morgue. No one will care. Life will move on as usual. Aunt Marie could be sad for a little bit I guess, but everyone knows she doesn't even like me. She shouldn't. I was always bad to her. I never trusted her. I don't regret these things, but they are my reality. This is how things are and this is how things were always going to be. I wasn't meant to live a full life. As long as I am here, someone else suffers. Who wants to live that kind of life. What kind of life is that? It is no life at all. Well not really. It is worse than that because at least when I am gone, I can't hurt anyone anymore. This is what is, and this is what it has to be.

And just like that she jumps.

No second thoughts.

No second guesses.

No regrets.

It's simple.

It's quick.

And that's that.

It's the end of her story.

Many things in her life didn't make sense up to that point, but she always did her best to piece it back together. It's a strange feeling. *I couldn't have jumped.* Her memory is still fuzzy at this particular moment, but as always, she does her best to pick up the pieces and mend them back together. *One more time...*

***

The sun shines through the window just like any other day. Despite all that happened last night, the sun still shines without fail.

Celest sits up and slowly cranes her head around the room. She's not really looking for anything. She eventually rests her eyes on Buddy who is standing next to her bed. He also looks back to her, noticing that she had awakened. Normally, Celest would point out how strange it was that Buddy had woken up before her, but she shrugs it off.

"Ready to go on your walk!?" she says excitedly to Buddy.

Buddy dances in place and smiles at her. He always loves going outside. Celest hasn't dedicated as much personal walking time for Buddy since her mom passed away. She replays the day that her and Evelyn went on a walk together repeatedly in her head. It is the only really good memory she has of her mom and her. *Why couldn't I just understand sooner?*

Celest fits Buddy's harness around his neck and onto the rest of his body. *A little snug...* Celest hasn't kept track of how much she has been walking Buddy recently, but it clearly isn't often enough. Buddy has put on a few pounds. It's nothing bad, but Celest needs to keep him healthy so he can keep her healthy. *Walking him is moving up on the priority list.* Buddy continues to bounce. He hasn't got a care in the world, which makes him and Celest similar in a way. *Do I not have a care in the world, or does the world not have a care about me?* She attaches his leash.

"I'm leaving out!" Celest shouts to the other side of the room.

Aunt Marie yells back, "Alright, be careful!"

Aunt Marie's voice almost makes Celest smile, but it doesn't quite get her there. She just nods in her head and continues for the door.

The sun is somber today. The homes are quiet and still. No birds are chirping. No kids are playing. It's just Celest and her dog, alone once again. *There is a strange comfort in being alone. I know that I would never reach out to someone to help me, so what really is my alternative? I was meant to be alone. Or maybe I wasn't, but somewhere along the way I came to know it as home.* Celest feels a slight tug in her hand. Buddy is trotting in front of her with his head held high. He stops to look at some squirrels that run by but continues trotting soon after.

The paved street soon fades into the battered dirt path that is engrained in Celest's memory. The atmosphere softens and the environment becomes more elegant and intriguing. Celest scans her environment as she usually does. Today she isn't really looking for anything, but she has a weird feeling that she will find something, or that something will find her. Something is a little bit off, maybe it is the scent of the woods or the way the sun shines through the trees. It's not clear, but *something is off. Today will be different.*

What is so different about this place? Celest cranes her head in all directions looking for some discrepancy, a continuity error, *something* to put her mind at ease. *The birds are more active today than usual. I can hear them zipping between the branches of the trees. They sing to each other so beautifully.*

Celest finds a nice tree to sit under as she stares up into the canopies. She stays there for a while observing the birds. Her faint smile eventually fades though. As pretty as they are, they're no different than they're supposed to be. They continue their daily routines as usual. *They are really remarkable creatures. They always seem happy. Always cheerful and singing. Always....the same.*

Buddy has made himself comfortable on the ground next to Celest. He seems to enjoy the birds as well.

He never chases them as most dogs might, but he just likes to watch as they fly around him. He watches them with Celest for a little while until he spots a deer drinking from the nearby pond.

Celest continues to stare at the sky. It's as if it is calling to her, wanting her to lose herself in it. Celest listens. She stares off and drifts from her body. There is only her and the sky. Nothing else matters. Celest has been drifting off like this a lot more often. She recognizes that she is very unaware of her surroundings now, losing her sense of time and misremembering events. Sometimes she would recite things to Aunt Marie only for her to look back at Celest with a genuinely confused stare. Things just don't really line up correctly for Celest right now. That doesn't scare her though. *Life isn't meant to make sense, right?*

***

The sun shines onto Celest through the trees. She pulls her head on top of her shoulders. Her neck and shoulders are aching from her resting position. She must not have been out for too long. If she was, Aunt Marie would have surely come to find her.

Through her grogginess, Celest can make out Buddy chasing some animals that are roaming around. She doesn't think much of it as she expects him to frolic around at least for some of his life. *It must be hard to be on duty all the time.* Instead of reprimanding him, she walks to the edge of the pond. A pair of frogs jumping across lily pads catches her eye. A small grin sneaks onto her face.

Celest pulls out her journal again. Out of everything that doesn't make sense in her life, her journal is a constant that she can always rely on. No matter where she is, the journal seems to follow. She turns to a new page and begins sketching the rough outline of two blobs moving between two different platforms. In the beginning the drawing doesn't make much sense, but Celest keeps at it. *The eyes, the mouth, some legs here......* Quickly her vision manifests on the page: two frogs chasing each other on lily pads.

Buddy has trotted over to Celest by the time she is finished sketching the frogs. He sits and watches them as well, equally entertained by their little game. Celest peaks over the edge of her notebook to smile at her dog. *It's nice to see him take a break.* Celest's smile doesn't have a chance to settle, however. Buddy can sometimes be impulsive, something conditioned out of him when he was trained as a service animal, but as Celest likes to put it, *a service dog is still a dog after all.* Before she has a chance to process what is about to happen, Celest is overcome with an overwhelming volume of water. Buddy had jumped into the pond.

"HEY!" a harsh voice rings out.

Celest whips her head around to face this mysterious voice. She can see someone sitting by the pond a little ways away from her and buddy. They are stiffened up like a wet cat. *Yikes... How did I not see them there?* Celest stiffens herself, not really enjoying interacting with random people. *I don't really like speaking to anyone at all...*

The person is wrapped up in a blue hoodie. It looks like they're small in comparison to Celest, but their attire adds some ambiguity to them. They slowly start to shake off the water that Buddy splashed them with. Seeing this, Celest awkwardly walks over to them.

"Hey...uh...Sorry about my dog..." she says with a forced smile.

As if on cue, Buddy hops out of the water and trots to Celest's side, trailing water behind him. Of course, he shakes himself dry which only drenches the stranger further. *No no no!* They don't really do anything. They look like they have just accepted defeat at this point.

Celest hastily apologizes, "Sorry!"

The stranger turns their head to Celest. Her expression is completely unamused. Her hair sticks to her forehead and her eyes stare Celest down. *Sorry...* In her panic, Celest doesn't notice how familiar the girl looks. She has soft freckles over her face and although she is annoyed, her eyes remain sort of unreadable.

Buddy ignores the tension between the two and plops down, right next to the girl. His tail wags furiously. The girl hovers her hand over his back contemplating if she should touch him. Eventually she decides that she will and rests her hand on Buddy.

This sight was really sweet, but Celest knows that she has to tell everyone that they can't pet Buddy because it distracts him from working. Most of the time she doesn't even tell people this though. *I don't need a service dog to survive.* She doesn't know this person though and it's an easy way to get out of this awkward situation, so she tries to use it as an excuse to leave.

"Um..I know you didn't know this," she says through a fake smile, "but he's my service animal, so you can't actually pet him because-"

"Well, you let me pet him before," the girl responds flatly, "And he just splashed me."

Before? The girl's soft voice sounds like a melody to Celest. *No way*. It is the girl from the art fair.

"Hey, I know you," Celest says in an accusatory tone.

The girl completely ignores her and just pets Buddy. *Okayy....?* Celest puts her hands on her hips and stares at the girl. She can't just ignore her like that. Celest continues to stare...and stare...and stare...but the girl continues to ignore her. It's like Celest isn't even there.

Suddenly though, the girl stands up and starts walking away from Celest. She is heading in the opposite direction that Celest came from. There must be another path down that way that Celest doesn't know about. Buddy circles back around to his owner. *Such a strange girl.*

After standing baffled, Celest yells in the girl's direction, "HEY! Where are you going? You're just going to leave like that?"

"Does it matter?" the girl softly answers, "I bet you don't even remember my name."

Celest is baffled by the girl's demeanor. She was nothing like this when she first met her. But to her credit, she is right. *I don't remember her name. Perry? Percy? No, it was unique. Just like me.* Celest takes hold of Buddy's leash and trails the girl. She awkwardly matches the girl's pace and walks next to her. Of course, the girl has no reaction at all and keeps walking to wherever she is going. It's not a good idea to follow her, but Celest just has a feeling about her. *I was meant to run into you today, wasn't I?*

Without any real reason, Celest decides not to ask the girl anything. Not a "Where are you going?" or a "What was your name again?" She is completely silent and just lets nature take its course. She lets her mind wander into the trees once again. There are deer and squirrels and birds all around them. The part of the woods they are entering is much denser than before, but Celest can hear a gravel path under them with every step she takes. *This is nice.*

The woods take her mind off of everything that has happened today. Or at least what she thinks happened today. *To be honest I don't remember much at all lately. Just what is and what isn't, but that gets blurry sometimes too. If life is what there is and what there isn't, shouldn't I not exist?* Celest can't shake the feeling that something happened to her recently. She shouldn't be here. *Something that would've prevented me from being here... Something that was in my control. Something that I chose. What did I do? I am here right? I'm not dreaming. This is real. But I don't feel real. I should not be here. But why should I not be here. I mean I exist. So, I should be here. But it's not right. I am out of place. I need to be back in place. I need to go back where I'm supposed to be. I need to be...*

The roof...

She needs to get back to the roof. She's not here. She's on the roof. But she can't be on the roof. She is here. Right? She is on the path that she walked with Evelyn. She is revisiting old memories today. She is doing better now. She is on the right path. She just is on a walk. She is on a walk with this girl that she met at the art fest. She has to be. But she jumped. So that means she's...

Celest stumbles on a tree root that is poking out of the ground. *What was I thinking?* She tries to shake her head a few times to get her mind right.

"You alright back there?" a voice asks her.

Celest answers without looking up, "Y-Yeah.. I'm alright..."

She looks down at her hands. She's shaking tremendously, but that's not what catches her eye. A faint glow emanates from her and connects her to her walking partner. The girl is still facing forward, so she isn't able to see it. Celest's eyes widen. She looks around her to see if anything is illuminating them, but she finds more questions than answers. The entire environment has been engulfed in an angelic light blue sky. The animals that run by have the same glow trailing them. *You heard me.* Celest quickens her pace to close the space between her and the girl. As she gets closer to her, the girl's name pops into her head. *Pepper. But that's not what you told me is it?*

Celest tucks her head and continues on the path. Whatever message is meant for her must be received through Pep. *I don't want to mess this up again.*

Eventually the grassy environment turns back into roads and the trees turn into houses. This place doesn't nearly resemble Aunt Marie's neighborhood at all. The street is made of red cobblestone and each house is bigger than the last. The smallest house that Celest can point out has to be a million *at least*. The outsides of the houses are decorated with fancy statues and glass art. A couple of them have fountains in the front yard. *Where are we?* The sky continues to glow, and it seems that it is only Celest and Pep around. It's almost reminiscent of an angel walking a soul up to the golden gates, but that can't be what is happening. After all, *I'm still alive.*

Pep speaks in her soothing voice, "My house is right there on the right." She points a few houses down.

Celest can't help but break her silence. "You live here!?" she exclaims.

Pep chuckles and nods her head. Once she is nearing her house, she pulls her hood off her head. Her straight, bright orange hair flows down her head. *Woah. That's new.*

Pep leads Celest all the way up to her front door. *It won't be hard to remember this house!* She immediately notices how large Pep's house is. It *must* be the biggest on the block. It also has many flowers decorating the outside of it like Aunt Marie's house. *Must be something about adults and flowers...* Pep simply turns and looks at Celest after arriving at her door.

"You know," Pep starts, "I was thinking earlier, and I thought it was a little strange that you never mentioned to me that you were having a birthday party."

What? Out of all things that she could say right now that's what she has to say? "Well.... that's because I'm not having one?" Celest responds.

Pepper looks confused. "Oh," she says, "I just assumed that you were because your birthday is coming up."

My birthday is coming up?

Pep notices Celest's expression and elaborates, "Your name was on the board that shows who has a birthday this month."

Right. Celest has never taken a liking to her art teacher's tradition of having a birthday wall of sorts. Everyone used to come up to her and wish her happy birthday, but Celest never wanted to hear those words. How can she ever celebrate? How can she celebrate when she doesn't even have anything to be happy about? She never understood it, but the other children in her class loved it, so she never complained to them. She simply nodded her head and went about her day. This seemed a bit off though. *Why now? How would you have noticed that?*

Celest gets lost in her thoughts again. This time they aren't really coherent. They're not sensical. It's almost as if she is trying to tell a story to herself that has missing plot points. The pieces don't exactly line up. The ends never tighten all the way. Even if Pep had known her name before she looked at the birthday wall, why would that have been a thing that she did? Why would that be her line of thought? It *could* make sense, but if she really thought about it, if she stopped and recited it to herself, start to finish, it quickly unravels.

Celest speaks as she lifts her head, "I...just don't quite under-" As soon as her eyes focus again, she realizes she is addressing an empty landscape. Only the decorated house and the trees look back at her.

Pepper is nowhere to be seen.

Chapter 11: Party for Three

My birthday...

Celest stares up at the ceiling. She is back home. Or at least she feels as if she is back home. She's not entirely sure that she's left this spot in a while. It wouldn't make sense. *Pep is real. I am real. All of it was real.* She keeps repeating things to herself to convince herself that her walk was normal and everything around her is just as it should be. If she said it enough, maybe she would believe it. It has worked for her before. *I'm not meant to be here....*

Aunt Marie is in the living room watching television. Celest can hear the faint voices of familiar characters arguing with each other. Aunt Marie loves watching soap operas, which Celest doesn't understand, but finds sweet. Buddy is laying down to the left of Celest's bed. He is patiently waiting for something to do. *Everything is fine...*

Celest mindlessly rolls out of her bed and approaches her door. Buddy joins her side quietly. *It's ok.* She grabs at the doorknob. When her door opens, she sees Aunt Marie stretched out on the couch watching the TV. Celest can feel herself staring intently at Aunt Marie, but she can't stop herself. Her face must resemble that of a ghost, or of someone who came down with the flu. Her soul just isn't all the way there.

"Did I go out yesterday?" Celest's voice says very strangely. It isn't scared. It isn't sick. It isn't happy or sad. It isn't warm. It might be described as cold, but that isn't exactly it.

It just *exists*.

Aunt Marie looks at Celest without turning her head from the TV. In a confused tone she says, "Yes?"

Celest continues to stare slightly to the side of Aunt Marie. *So, I did go on a walk yesterday. It did happen. I'm not crazy. I'm perfectly normal. I'm-*

"You always go out to walk your dog…" Aunt Marie interrupts.

Celest responds, "Right… and the girl…"

Aunt Marie turns away from the television entirely to study Celest. "Are you ok?" she asks.

Celest nods briefly before taking an awkward step backwards and shutting her door once again. *Birthday….* Celest stumbles to her bed, catching herself with her hands. Her heart pounds and her breathing is shallow. Suddenly she throws herself at her dresser. Buddy watches in confusion as Celest tears her clothes out each drawer. One compartment at a time, Celest empties her wardrobe onto the floor. A sea of colors stream over Buddy's head. Some of the clothes land on his head, but he just shakes them off and waits patiently. It is a very odd site. She is looking for something, but what is it?

Got it. Celest's manic episode appears to stop not too long after it starts. At the bottom of the lowest drawer there is an opened envelope. It must've been buried there for a while. Celest holds it up to her face as if it is a sacred item. The original letter is still inside. She reads over it again and again.

Imani

-

Hangout

Hello. I know this is a little awkward, but I wanted to ask if maybe I could come over sometime in the next few weeks. My parents don't let me out much, but I'm sure I could figure out a way for them to let me come over. Or I'll find a day where they're not home. I don't know. We don't have to. I was just wondering.

Perfect! Celest looks at the calendar hanging on her wall. *Right on time.* Celest can feel the corners of her mouth upturn and that fleeting feeling of excitedness. *When's the last time that happened?* She thinks to herself for a moment, but she shakes it off. With Imani's letter in hand, Celest struts back into the living room. Aunt Marie looks beyond confused at her behavior. She doesn't say anything to Celest either out of her choice or simply because she is at a loss for words. Buddy trots to Aunt Marie to give her kisses while Celest fades into the hallway.

Blue, purple, white. Celest flips on the light of the art room. For the first time in a while, she is happy. She has something to do with herself. She is going to make *birthday invitations.* Two to be exact. Aunt Marie has an art stand that always has extra things in it: extra paintbrushes, extra paper, and random trinkets. Celest digs around in it until she finds two unused envelopes and paper that she can make her cards out of. She decides to use parchment so she can paint on them without withering the pages.

Pink? No that wouldn't fit. Celest sits in front of an easel. *It's easier to paint like this than if it were laying down. She* begins working. She mixes her colors and gets a general sense of what she wants her art to look like. *It should flow like water. The blue can look like the sea, the white the foam, and the purple like the sunset.* The paint flows over the pages and blends into marvelous colors.

They're all interconnected. *We're always interconnected. Never alone, just a page away. No one is alone. They are just one page away. I am a page away from my destination.*

Soft hums fill the room. Periodically they will stop when she needs a moment to concentrate, but otherwise her hums ring true. Aunt Marie is intrigued by Celest's sudden bliss. She sits up on the couch before creeping down the hall. She peaks her head into the art room as if she was assigned to spy on Celest. Her eyes are wide. Celest is enjoying herself. She is enjoying something. Aunt Marie frames the rest of her body in the doorway and allows herself to be in awe. She considers asking what Celest is doing but decides not to ruin the moment.

In no time, Celest finishes her little project and claims her victory with a fist pump into the air. She prepares her envelopes while she waits for the paint to dry. *Imani and Pep. Birthday invitations.* All that was left to do is wait.

Finding the courage to ask, Aunt Marie almost whispers, "Celest, what are you doing?"

Huh? Celest turns to look at Aunt Marie. She is standing as if she had seen a ghost. *Are you alright?* "I was just painting," Celest responds.

Aunt Marie responds stiffly, "Oh...ok.."

What is up with her?

"You just decided to...?" Aunt Marie continues.

I like painting. I have always painted. Why is that so weird?

"Well, I guess not," Celest says, "I wanted to make birthday cards."

Aunt Marie is almost frozen in place. Her entire being is stiff and her eyes bulge out of her head. She loosely resembles a zombie. Mechanically, she takes a couple paces forward, so she is right in front of Celest. She places her arms around Celest and hugs her. She doesn't speak a word, but Celest can feel her emotion. *When was the last time I hugged someone?*

Celest does not move. *What am I supposed to do?* Her arms hang awkwardly to her side. She can feel Aunt Marie's heartbeat against her own. It's strong and steady, much like Aunt Marie herself. Celest has never seen Aunt

Marie react to her like this. *When I really think back, she's not a very touchy person.*

After a while, Aunt Marie pulls back, but leaves her hands on Celest's shoulders. She looks at Celest with something foreign in her eyes. *She's crying. Why is she crying?* Celest stares at her. *She's never cried before...* She tries to come up with something that will put Aunt Marie at ease, or at least distract her from whatever is troubling her.

"...I thought that I should have a little get together for my birthday...if that's ok," she stammers.

Aunt Marie just smiles at Celest. "Yes, of course you can," she says while tears fall down her face.

She pulls Celest in again. This time, neither of them say a word. They just stand in embrace. *An embrace long overdue.* Celest focuses on Aunt Marie's heartbeat. *There is so much comfort in being held by someone. We aren't speaking, but she's saying everything. This embrace is warm...which is nice. But I can't help but wonder if there is another person hugging both of us now.*

***

"I'll be back soon!" Celest exclaims as she closes the front door.

Aunt Marie is more than happy to let Celest hand deliver her letters. It is rare that Celest asks to do anything, let alone to go see anyone, so this is a pleasant surprise.

Buddy is in his harness, skipping alongside Celest. He smiles at her as she gives him a small pat on his head. "Alright," Celest says, "Don't drop those, ok?" Celest puts the two letters in the side of Buddy's harness. He stares at her while she does so, but it doesn't bother him.

Celest holds her journal in her left hand. Before she starts walking, she takes a second to write down her friends' names. *Imani and Pep.* She doesn't know why she wanted to write them down. She knows where she is going. *It's nice to look at I suppose.* She begins walking down her driveway in the direction of Imani's house. *I have to see her first.*

Celest gets lost in her journal as she walks. *I haven't even tried to contact her in how long? I don't remember the last time she has been over. It must be because I am so busy with school though. I wouldn't just leave her like that. Of course not. She's one of my best friends. Well, my only real friend really. The people at school don't really care like she does. Which is another reason why I would always want to see her. Right?*

Before she knows it, she is standing in front of a familiar decorated door. *That was quicker than usual...* The greenery around the house looks absolutely beautiful. There are perfectly manicured bushes lining the sides of the house, directing visitors to the porch. The small porch is bleach white and adorns a few hanging flowerpots. Everything looks perfect; even the grass grows a little greener at Imani's house. Celest traces her hand around the embordered door frame. *I'd be nice to live here.*

She knocks on the door. *You know, this house does look a bit out of place with all these decorations... It never dawned on me before, but all of these things are black and white. The flowers, the door and frame, the porch...All of it is bleak. It's fancy, but it's missing something. It doesn't feel like home. It's just a house.* She knocks again.

"Hello!" she calls out this time, "Imani, are you home?"

My voice sounds weird. When's the last time I spoke like that? Celest waits a few more seconds. *I guess not*. She turns to leave but remembers something that Imani told her randomly one day. Celest was asking her how to reach her if she wasn't home. Imani simply responded to wait at her house. *Just check the front.*

Celest checks her surroundings. She can't get caught snooping into someone's house, especially this *nice* house, and especially because she looks like she does. She looks back at the doorknob. Shakily, she wraps her hand around it. *Ok. Here goes nothing.* She quickly turns her hand to the side, closing her eyes as she does so. *Huh?* The knob doesn't budge. It's locked. *Of course, it's locked...Why wouldn't it be?* Celest sighs.

Maybe a different entrance? She swiftly looks around the porch but doesn't see anything unusual. *Just a window and a door. Nothing else. Some bushes and then the backyard I'm assuming.* Celest stares at the window for a quick second, not long enough for someone to notice, but too long for it to be a glance. *The window...* She walks over and tries to open it. *As if that will work.* There's a satisfying *shhhwooop. No way.*

The window is big enough for her to fit through, but there is no way that she would hop into these people's houses. She's been taught better than that. She ops instead to take Imani's letter and put it through the window. The letter drops and hits the hardwood floor on the other side. Once it is delivered, Celest slides the window closed again. *Why would she just leave that open?*

She tries not to dwell on it for too long. She does make a note of it in her journal though. *Ask Imani about the open window.* Celest peeks at Buddy and winks at him. He barks at her in response. "Alright next stop, Pep's house!" she says to him. They leave Imani's house and go back to the main road. Celest still checks over her shoulders periodically until they are completely out of range.

They make their way to the woods' entrance. The trees are as green as ever this time of year. The sound of animals running around comforts Celest. *I'm never alone, you're just a page away.* She closes her eyes and imagines that ethereal walk she had yesterday. She takes a deep breath. *I remember the sky and how it glowed. The leaves of the trees blew in the wind. You showed me the path before, I need to see it again.* As if on cue, a breeze kicked up around Celest. The wind speaks to her in a quiet howl. She slowly opens her eyes to see the dreamlike world she was in before. The sky is filled with pretty blues, purples, and pinks. The animals line up on either side of one of the trails and look at Celest, guiding her in the right direction. *Thank you.*

Celest follows the trail of animals down winding paths through the woods. *Her house must be on the other side of the woods entirely.* Unlike last time, she can really take in the sight around her. The animals have a faint green glow, and their eyes are completely white. In a different context, Celest would've been afraid, but she is comforted by the fact that *someone* is watching over her. *This all has to be happening for a reason. It has to be.*

Aside from the dreamy scene, the walk was very repetitive. She enjoys looking around as she travels until the path transitions back into asphalt. The sky fades back to summer blue and the animals retreat into the woods. It's just Celest and Buddy now. *That house on the right.*

Celest approaches Pep's house. It doesn't look as majestic as before, but it's recognizable. She raises her hand to knock on the door like she did at Imani's house but lowers it as she sees a doorbell to her left.

Riiiiingggg!

Celest bends down to pet Buddy while she waits for someone to answer the door. His tail wags on the ground. *You've always loved attention.* She loves to love up on Buddy sometimes because he is always working. *He deserves some attention.*

"Can I help you?"

What?!

Celest quickly stands up and turns around startled. There is a short woman peering at her from inside the house. She has jet black hair and is wearing a sports cap. Celest can't see her body very well but based on her face and her arm holding the door open, she is petite.

Celest fumbles over her words, spewing out a flurry of I's, um's, and oh's. The woman looks even more confused at her. *She is going to think I am crazy!* She continues to fumble over herself as she frantically reaches in Buddy's harness and pulls Pep's letter out. She practically throws it at the woman and bows her head in shame. *That was awful.*

The woman looks Celest up and down again. She still looks at her strangely but accepts the letter. She flips it over to see "PEP" in large letters on the envelope. She closes the door, taking the letter with her.

Celest looks up. She can hear presumably the lady yell in another language behind the door. Not long after the door opens again, and this time Pep is standing in the doorway. She greets Celest with a huge smile. Celest thought Pep might've wanted to give her a hug, but she never made any attempt to get closer to her. *Maybe it's just not her thing.*

Pep closes the front door behind her. Still, smiling, she opens Celest's letter. *That lady must've been her mother. But the hair...* Celest tries to think of anything but the fact that Pep is opening her card right in front of her. *I thought I could just drop it off and leave. I didn't know I was going to have to wait and see if she rejects me or not.*

Pep says in a teasing tone, "I thought you weren't having a party?"

Celest responds matter-of-factly, "Well I wasn't, but now I am."

Pep chuckles, which is strange to Celest. *I don't think she's ever been this happy before. I guess that's going around...* Celest doesn't try and stick around any longer than she has to. She weirdly turns to leave. *Mission accomplished.*

"You don't want to stay any longer?" Pep asks with a bit of sadness in her voice.

Celest turns back around and puts on a smile. *This was not part of my plan.* "Sure," she forces out. *You don't even know me that well...*

Pep excitedly reopens her front door and motions for Celest to come in. Celest follows her inside. The interior of the house is huge. It looks big on the outside, but on the inside it's humongous. *You could land a helicopter here.* The ceilings are so tall that they might as well reach the sky. It looks like they are in the living room. The kitchen is to the left.

Celest bumps into Pep as she is mindlessly walking forward. *Sorry.* Pep doesn't seem to mind. In fact, she might've stopped there on purpose. They were only a little ways into the house. Pep points to an area of shoes behind Celest. She looks at them but doesn't understand. She then peers down to see if something was wrong with her shoes. Instead, she sees that Pep is in her socks. *You want me to take my shoes off?* She doesn't really understand, but she complies with the house rules. She slides her shoes off and lines them up with the others.

Pep asks Celest to wait on the living room couch for a moment and then leaves the room. She sits and Buddy lays on the floor in front of her. She sinks into the comfortable couch cushions. Pep reenters the room with the woman who was at the door and a man of a similar stature. He also has jet black hair. Pep highly resembles the man. *That must be dad.*

Celest gets up when she sees the adults enter the room. Pep motions to Celest and says, "This is the girl I always talk about. And these," she motions to the two adults, "are my parents."

"Nice to meet you," Celest says while she extends a hand.

Both of Pep's parents look at Celest's hand but don't shake it. Her mom faintly smiles and nods to Celest. Her dad does the same. *Her parents must be quiet too.* Pep's mom peers over the couch at buddy and smiles at him. Surely, he would smile back at her, but he was fast asleep. After this short interaction, Pep's parents disappear into the house again.

Pep looks at Celest with a smile. "So," she says, "Those are my parents."

Yeah...

Pep mumbles, "I just wanted you to meet them before you left."

Thank goodness. Celest takes that comment as her ticket to freedom. She can leave the house. She grabs Buddy's leash and gives it a gentle tug to wake him up.

"Well, thank you for wanting to go to my party," she says.

Pep responds excitedly, "Of course!"

Celest slips her shoes back on and readjusts them with her fingers.

"So, I'll see you tomorrow then?" Celest asks.

"I'll see you tomorrow!" Pep assures.

Chapter 12: D'etre

"So, what are some things you like to do in your spare time?"

The easiest way for Pep to reach Celest's house was for her to walk her there. Celest never gave her address out to anyone except for Imani, and even then, she didn't feel great about Imani knowing where she lives at first. It is easy for her to make her way back to Pep's house this time. She knew the path well enough to get there on her own, no divine intervention needed.

Pep is quick to come out of her house after she answers the door. As she is trying to leave, her mom bombards her with questions and some other things that Celest can't understand. *This must be her first time out like this.* She also carries a comically large bag on her that Celest is confused by, but decides not to question.

There is a noticeable breeze swaying the trees. This time of year, that can only mean that a storm is coming in the near future. Though, at least for now, it provides a comforting atmosphere for their walk. The animals aren't frolicking around at this time. Most of them are still sleeping or are resting in the grass. Buddy is sluggish as well, dragging his feet as he walks. *Sorry for waking you up so early.*

Celest thinks of all the things she likes to do when she's not at school. *Paint, draw, read, write...* She opens her mouth to tell Pep about the several hobbies she has but stops herself. *When's the last time I really did any of that?* Of course, Celest carries her journal everywhere, but she doesn't use it nearly as much as she could. It's filled with odd entries and little notes. Nothing consistent and nothing worth much. *I could say reading....* But she can't even remember the last time she picked up a book. Her collection sits in her room collecting dust. *Painting and drawing then...* Even telling Pep that she makes art in her free time wouldn't be completely true. She made the birthday cards yesterday, but *Aunt Marie looked ghost white* while she was doing so.

"Me?" she says as if she's surprised, "I sit around and paint canvases. I take Buddy out and play with him sometimes too."

Pep buys her story, or at least if she doesn't, she's good at hiding it. "That's nice," she responds with a smile, "My family doesn't have pets, but there's a stray cat that likes to hang out near our pool. I play with her when she comes out."

Celest decides to return the question back to her friend: "What do you do in your free time?"

Pep grins from ear to ear. "Well, I like to play tennis, I play the piano, and I compete in math competitions!" she says gleefully.

Math competitions? Celest can't imagine herself ever going to one of those. It's not like she isn't a smart kid; she is one of the top students in her grade. Math just isn't something she can ever do in her free time. *It's so frustrating!* But, if that's what makes Pep happy, more power to her.

The rest of their stroll goes a lot like this conversation. One of them asks a question and the other answers. It's not the most productive conversation, but they did get to learn some things about each other. Pep has an older brother who is off in college. He is very accomplished and got into a prestigious university. Her family goes to China to visit her grandparents every so often. Her parents immigrated to the U.S. which explains what other language they speak. Pep prides herself in school. She doesn't seem to have much of a social life. *Such an interesting life. I wish my family was as strong as yours.* She also tells Celest that the bag she is carrying is full of food from her mother and chuckles while saying that her mother isn't too fond of her hair color.

Celest stays as engaged in the conversation as she can without feeling down about herself. She shares her love of art and how she is a good student. She tells Pep of her condition and why she has Buddy. Other than that, she just listens to what Pep has to say.

Eventually the canopies of the trees no longer hang overhead. The gravel becomes a road and houses appear in front of them. Celest leads Pep to the front door. Pep looks around at Aunt Marie's various flowers and even squats down to touch a few lining the path to the door. Buddy jumps in front of both of them. He sits and wags his tail wildly awaiting what's inside. Celest rings the doorbell.

Aunt Marie's voice sounds faintly through the door: "Coming!"

Within a few moments the door softly swings open. Celest is immediately hit with the smell of Aunt Marie's cooking. It's warm and inviting, more so than usual. *Maybe she decided to make something different today.* Buddy invites himself inside by squeezing himself between Aunt Marie's legs. Celest lets his harness go.

"This is Pep," Celest explains while gesturing to her friend, "I met her in art this year. She lives in the next neighborhood over."

Aunt Marie nods at Pep and gives an introduction of her own: "Nice to meet you Pep. You can call me Aunt Marie."

Aunt Marie doesn't really give Pep a tour of the house or really say much to either of them after that. She simply lets them in the house and gets back to cooking. *What am I supposed to do now?* Celest was relying on the fact that Aunt Marie enjoys talking. In the time that she would finish with Pep, maybe Celest could've thought of something to do with her, but now they're just standing in the living room. *What do people usually do when they have parties at their houses?*

Celest silently panics. She does her best to hide her nervousness by looking around the room, which probably makes her look even more nervous, but Pep doesn't notice. She is busy looking around the unfamiliar space and watching Aunt Marie work in the kitchen. Celest happens to look towards her room door, which is slightly open. She spots one of her paintings hanging on her wall and gets an idea. *Now that's something we can do.*

Still glancing into her bedroom, she asks, "Hey Pep, you want to paint something?"

"Do you mean to decorate for your party?" Pep questions back.

Decorate? What part of what I just said made it sound like I wanted to decorate? Celest looks puzzled for a moment, but an image of Pep's house pops into her mind. In the living room of Pep's house there are several canvases hung all over the walls. She didn't really note it while she was there, but *Pep's family must make their own home decorations.* She decides to just go with it.

"Yeah. I thought it would be nice to decorate the place," she says.

Celest tells Pep to follow her to her room. She goes to her art drawer and picks out a few blank banners that she hasn't used yet. She wraps them around her arms and then opens another section of the drawer to grab a bunch of paint brushes. She zips back and forth between the living room and her room, picking up and dropping off art supplies.

Pep stands just outside her room door. She never steps foot in Celest's room, but she does look in awe of all the paintings she can see on Celest's walls. Every last corner has some sort of art in it from sketches to clay sculptures. She can't help but feel a little jealous of her friend's talent, but she also feels overwhelmingly proud of her.

Pep stops Celest the next time she zooms past her and asks, "Did you paint those?"

Celest responds out of breath, yet not stopping, "Yes! Do you like them!?"

"I think they're amazing," Pep concludes.

Pep sits on the living room rug until Celest is done bringing out her supplies. When she is done, she takes a big breath. *Alright that has to be enough stuff.* In hindsight, she overkills the number of things she brings out. She extends both of her arms out as to say, *"Let's get started!"*

Pep and Celest select what they want to use on the banner and huddle it near themselves. Celest chooses her usual colors, a mix of purple to blue. *There's something about that color spectrum that is just really calming. I feel like it represents myself. The deep blues represent the valleys, and the purple represents the mountains, but all of them are subtle. They don't pop out at you immediately. Their beauty is in their intricacy.*

Pep selects an entirely different set of colors. Her choices are more muted colors like brown and grey. She uses pops of colors such as gold and orange occasionally. Those are reserved for focus points in her art. She also has a different art process than Celest. She doesn't pick up any sketching tools. It seems she just knows what she is going to paint before it hits the page.

She begins painting the right side of the banner, farthest away from Celest. Celest finds some skill in being able to paint like this. *She's going backwards...* Despite Celest's curiosity, Pep seems to be completely comfortable in her art style. She makes her way from right to left just as Celest makes her way left to right. She decides to start on her side so Pep doesn't get too far ahead of her.

About thirty minutes into their activity, Pep asks, "So, who else is coming to the party?"

"My friend Imani should be coming, and I passed out some other letters as well..." Celest returns.

Pep doesn't visibly acknowledge her answer and continues to paint. After some time, there's a knock at the door. Buddy dashes towards the noise. Celest begins to clean her hands off to answer it, but Aunt Marie makes her way to the door before she can finish doing so. She answers the door as she did before.

Imani walks into the living room wearing sweatpants and a T-shirt. She looks much less shy than the last time Celest remembers seeing her and she actually talks to Aunt Marie for a little while. After giving Imani a proper greeting, Aunt Marie walks to her room. *Weren't you cooking?* Celest wonders why Aunt Marie doesn't return to the kitchen, but when she looks over, the food is now laid out on the kitchen table.

Celest stands to give Imani a hug but makes sure not to touch Imani with her hands. "Long time no see!" Celest exclaims.

It feels strange to have them in the house. It's a nice feeling, but it makes me uneasy. It makes me feel like something is about to happen to someone. I guess that's how I think because of things that have happened before. I shouldn't think like that right? I shouldn't feel that way. What could possibly happen? Nothing could happen right? Nothing at all. Everything will be fine. I really need to stop thinking like this, but I can't help but feel that there is a reason I do.

"Earth to Celest."

Huh?

Imani is looking at Celest like she has three eyes.

"Oh! Sorry..." Celest says, embarrassed.

I must've been staring at her. Celest points in the direction of Pep and the banner spread out on the ground. She follows up with, "This is what we've been doing. I'm painting the left side and she is painting the right. You could join in the middle if you want. There's still some space left."

Imani gently declines her offer: "Thanks but I'm not much of an artist. I could paint some stick figures for you, but I don't think they would fit in."

They both laugh at Imani's idea. "Well," Celest says, "Would you like to watch?"

Imani accepts this proposal: "Sure."

Celest gets back in her spot on the floor and Imani sits behind her and Pep. Celest reorganizes her things so she can continue painting.

"This is Pep by the way. I met her at school," she makes sure to mention.

Imani and Pep exchange short hellos. For the next hour, Imani watches as the banner brims with color. The sea of colors from Celest's side clashes with Pep's muted scheme, but in the middle they create something entirely new. They mix their art together and create a gradient between the left and right sides of the banner. The middle is a transition from one side to the other. It's not seamless, but it's not meant to be. *It's just perfect.*

They leave the banner to dry on the tile floor. Imani points out that they should push the living room rug back so the paint doesn't seep through to the carpet. *Aunt Marie would not be happy about that.* All three of them carefully lift the banner out of the way and set it in the hallway. They then lift up one side of the carpet and fold it back under the couch. Lastly, they move the banner back to the living room.

That was nice. This is actually nice. All of this is. I'm having fun. I'm having a normal day around my friends. This is how it should always be. Why couldn't I do this before? Well, I know why. I can't let this take my mind too far from reality. This is temporary. It always is.

Celest decides to eat. The food is cold at this point, so she takes each plate that Aunt Marie made and warms it up in the microwave. She gives Pep and Imani their food before serving herself. *It's just something I've always been taught.* They all sit at the kitchen table and begin to eat. Aunt Marie had made ribs and rice, something Celest rarely got the chance to eat, but has always loved. Pep pulls out a small food container from the big bag her mom gave her and also eats what's in there along with Aunt Marie's dish.

Celest gets lost in conversation with her two friends as they talk and laugh throughout their meal. *It's almost as if we'll always be here. It's as if we can do this again. It's as if this isn't the end. It isn't a last-ditch effort to preserve what has already been lost. It's as if-*

It doesn't have to end.

***

By the late hours of the day, Aunt Marie has gone to the hospital for work and the three friends find themselves hanging out in Celest's room. Celest is showing them each and every canvas that she has painted up to this point and explaining what each means. Pep and Imani are sitting with their backs up against Celest's bed. Buddy is laying in front of both of them, enjoying the pets he's receiving.

Celest darts to each painting that Pep and Imani point out until there are no more left. She does one final scan of the room to make sure she covers everything. *That's everything.*

Imani looks at Celest's art drawer. "Do you ever make anything you don't like?" she asks, "I was just wondering because I never keep any of my art. It always ends up in the trash."

Without hesitation Celest answers, "Of course. Most of the paintings I make I don't particularly care for, or I think something isn't perfect about them." She doesn't hang on her answer and instead looks outside her window at the sun setting. "I think we should start wrapping up," she suggests.

She waltzes out of her room to check on the banner her and Pep made earlier. As she is walking out, she nonchalantly calls out, "I keep my unfinished and unpleasing canvases under my bed if you want to pull them out and look at them." She turns out of the room and goes to the banner.

It looks like it's dry... Celest pokes different portions of the banner to make sure none of the paint comes off. After checking the most paint-saturated spots, Celest picks up the top corner of her side of the painting and lifts the banner on its side. It tells an entirely different story when it's held vertically. It still clashes, but it looks like an ascension into the heavens. Celest's colorful sky covers the ground below in a mystical light. She stands and admires the banner. *Now this is a piece of art.*

Imani and Pep come out of Celest's room after looking through all the paintings under her bed. They both smile at her and tell her how they think the paintings weren't bad at all. *Sure.* Celest just nods at them and turns her attention back to the banner. *Where could I hang this one?*

Pep and Imani look over the art for a moment before starting to gather their things. Pep repacks her food bag first, which has been sitting in the refrigerator for a while. Imani begins to gather up the paint brushes even though she didn't use them. All the while, Celest thinks of what to do with the banner.

Eventually, Celest sets the banner down and returns the living room rug to its original position. The paint didn't bleed through the banner, but it was a nice idea to not let it sit on the rug. She is glad she didn't risk Aunt Marie being upset over her rug being soiled. After replacing the rug, she starts taking the brushes, stencils, and other materials back to her room. With all three of them working together, it doesn't take long for the room to get cleaned up.

Celest leads Pep and Imani towards the door and talks with them some more before ultimately, they have to leave to make it back home before sundown. Pep leaves first saying that her mother would hate her to not be in by sundown. She excuses herself and makes her way out. Celest and Imani give their goodbyes but stay a few minutes longer.

While she's on her way out the door, Imani quickly reaches into her pocket. "Oh!" she says, "I forgot to show you this." She reveals a small white envelope with nothing written on it. "I found this under your bed as well. I didn't read it, but it seems important, and I thought you maybe forgot about it," she continues.

Oh...

Celest feels a hole open in her stomach. She forces herself to take the note from Imani and to force a thankful smile. Imani waits for a thank you from Celest, but noticing her silence, she nods and turns to leave. Celest stares blankly at Imani walking away from the house. She can slowly feel herself coming back to her reality. *It's just a futile attempt to preserve something that's already gone. I'm already gone.*

When she reaches the road, Imani turns back to Celest with a big smile and yells, "I can't wait for the next party!"

The next party. There is no next party. This is it. This is me going out with a bang. Why don't they get it? This is it. This is the last time they will see me. I have gone on this long and it's coming to a close. This is my final chapter.

But it doesn't have to be.

Celest stares out into the neighborhood. *There's nothing left for me to do. This is all that my life has culminated too. I'll finally be happy. I'll finally be free.*

She's conflicted. She feels a battle going on in her entire being. Something in there is telling her that it's worth it. But why? All this time she has been content with the fact that this party is a great thing to do before going. Truth be told, she's not sure how she made it to this point. Something wants her to be here in this moment. But why?

Celest stares down at the note in her hand. *My final goodbye.* She gets a strange feeling in her throat. It almost feels like choking, but not quite. *I'm afraid.* The note in her hands feels like it's on fire, burning through her skin. *When's the last time I felt like that?*

Fear. She strangely smiles. *I'm afraid.* As if she is a ghost, Celest mindlessly wanders back into the house. She doesn't have much emotion or thought behind it, she just opens the door and wanders in. She continues to her room where she starts looking around.

All this time I have been looking forward to the end. All this time I have been waiting for something to take me out. I have dreamed about it. I have had hallucinations of it. Through all of it someone wanted me to stay here. Someone kept me here long enough to make me realize what I was doing. Someone was looking out for me.

She continues to search.

I never thought I would make it this far, and I didn't really have a reason to until you showed me. Yes, my life hasn't been the greatest, but that doesn't mean that I can't be someone for other people. Yes, I'm broken, but that doesn't mean I'm worthless. I can be someone to other people, even if I'm not here for myself.

She reaches behind a standing picture frame she has on top of her drawer. She feels around the area as it is too tall for her to see.

I will not give up on this. I won't give up on them. I have a purpose now. I must be here for my friends. It's not a grand reason to be alive, but it's my reason to live. I have to be there for them. If I'm not there, they will end up just as I was.

She grabs hold of a small lighter, no bigger than a pocketknife and examines it.

I know that it is you who has been guiding me this whole time. I can tell it's you up there in the clouds. Even when you're not here, you still try to protect me the best you can. I should've done more for you as you have done for me. This next chapter is for you mom. I will make you proud.

I held my lighter in one hand and my letter in the other. I felt tears welling in my eyes anticipating the relief I was about to feel. For the first time in years, I was going to be happy. I would be *alive*. I sparked the lighter with a satisfying *click*. I touched the flame to the paper, and I smiled as it burned.

I chose to live, not because I found a divine purpose, but because of two friends that I met in the right place at the right time. They were and still are worth living for.

About the Author

Riane Zháne Williams is an 18-year-old, black, Type 1 Diabetic, college student from Tallahassee, Florida. She has always loved learning about the world around her and prides herself on her prestigious academic achievements. Due to her unwavering ambition, she was able to graduate high school a year early with Summa Cum Laude status. Now, she is enjoying her sophomore year of college at Florida State University. Riane is the first student to pursue a dual bachelor's degree in Public Health and Chinese at FSU. She has continued receiving prestigious academic awards and is on a pre-medical track with intentions of getting a dual master's degree in Public Health and East Asian Languages: Chinese – another first at FSU. Her end goal is to obtain a dual MD/PhD degree, specializing in a primary care field and as a Doctor of Linguistics.

Riane began writing her debut novel in 8th grade (2018) with the intention of bringing more public attention to the chronic condition she suffers from, Type 1 Diabetes, and to shed light on childhood traumas. Growing up, she faced many struggles with depression and anxiety on top of learning how to live independently with an infamously deadly disease. Riane is very passionate about sharing stories with characters that have similar experiences to hers because she has struggled to find books with main characters that experience life through a similar lens. *Celest: Every Day is Closer to the End* aims to create a realistic and relatable story that accurately represents Type 1 Diabetes and the struggles of growing up in constant turmoil.

Made in the USA
Columbia, SC
26 September 2024

1c7554a2-4bea-4d99-bd20-4c3a9272451aR01